I dedicate this book to my family for their

encouragement and support.

Special thanks to my sons Tom and Jon and my writer friends in

Nashville and Maine.

Cover illustration by Tom Gammans

Halloran
Publishing

ISBN-13: 978-0615952499

ISBN-10: 0615952496

STORY STONES

Thea Gammans

 Halloran Publishing

BALLYDARE

THE WEST COAST OF IRELAND

1881

CHAPTER 1

The first time I heard the name Delia, I was six years old and sitting under the table listening to my grandmother read letters for the neighbors. The news their children sent from America was as fascinating as the stories Gran read to me from books.

When Gran left the room Mrs. Laughlin whispered, "Poor Nora. All these years and never a word from her daughter. T'is a heart of stone Delia Reardon must have not to write to her own mother."

I sat up straighter. Gran had a daughter named Delia!

Mrs. Boyle whispered back, "Strange how Delia hasn't kept in touch with a living soul in Ballydare."

"That girl always did set herself apart with her fine airs, like she was one of the gentry," Mrs. Laughlin replied.

Mrs. Boyle must have remembered that I was under the table. "Little pitchers have big ears," she cautioned. They talked about the weather until Gran came back in.

The reading continued but I no longer listened. How could a daughter be so mean that she didn't write to her mother? With my knees tucked under my chin, I stayed under the table, picturing Delia as one of the ugly stepsisters in Cinderella

I spent the rest of the day being especially good, so Gran would know she had a granddaughter who loved her, and never mentioned what the neighbors said because I was afraid it would make Gran sad.

It was six years before I heard the name Delia again, on a day, and in a way, that would change my life forever.

∞

After a week of rain, on what promised to be a perfect mid-summer day, Gran and I had spread sheets on the high grass to dry. As they whitened in the sun, I tossed crumbs and scraps to the geese and watched a steamship slip over the horizon.

I was counting the puffy clouds it left behind, and thinking of the grand adventures the passengers must be looking forward to when the geese set up a terrible honking and flapping of wings.

Recognizing the stout figure waddling down the road, I flung the last handful of crumbs to the ground and ran inside.

"Gran, Mrs. Laughlin must have a rare bit of news. She's coming like there's a strong wind behind her."

"News of somebody's troubles, Mary, or she's needing me to read a letter." My grandmother ran her fingers through her thin white hair, and removed her apron as our nearest neighbor made her way through the hissing and squawking.

From the door sill Hannah Laughlin called in, "Nora, Father Sheehy wants you and Mary to come to Saint Brigid's. He's had word from America." Her small, shrewd eyes swept every corner of the room as she added with a sly smile, "Perhaps it's your Delia writing, at long last."

My grandmother, a full head taller than Mrs. Laughlin, raised herself taller still. "Thank you for bringing the message, Hannah," she said coolly. There was no polite and expected invitation to come in. Mrs. Laughlin's remark had hurt.

As Mrs. Laughlin left she called over her shoulder, "After you've spoken with Father, I hope you and Mary drop by to share a cup and a biscuit."

"Thank you, but we'll probably come straight home." Gran's tone was still cool. "It's more than tea and a biscuit that one would be sharing," she mumbled as our neighbor retreated down the dusty road. "All Ballydare would buzz with any news I told her."

For a full minute she stood in the doorway and gazed at the sparkling harbor. Then she turned. "It's probably a letter for me from Annie Doyle in Liverpool. And Father's brought you a bit of reading from Galway. Change into your good dress, Mary."

My grandmother put on the black dress she'd bought when my grandfather died three years before. While she combed and tucked pins in her hair, I struggled into shoes that were growing tight, knowing I was never to be seen barefoot in the village.

As we walked the long shore road to Saint Brigid's, Gran's mouth was clamped tight, reminding me of Grandda's last days, when he'd smoked his long-stemmed clay pipe by the turf fire with little to say. By the time we'd gone half way, she was breathing heavily.

"Let's sit a bit," I suggested, and pointed to the large smooth rock I'd named the story stone because for as long as I could remember Gran had told me stories as we rested there.

"I'm not tired," she protested.

"But I feel a pebble in my shoe." I sat and shook out a bit of dust. My grandmother remained standing. She'd be telling no story today. Whatever news had come from America worried her.

As usual, we walked a bit faster past the long drive curving up to what people called the Big House, although the few times Gran mentioned it she called it Ashmont. Once when I asked if we could walk up to see the Big House, her "no" had been so sharp I never asked again.

By the edge of the village, Gran was catching her breath every few seconds. She barely slowed down to exchange a brief greeting with my teacher, Mrs. Dinsmore. I was disappointed.

Like everyone in Ballydare, I liked the Dinsmores. They were Quakers who had come to help during the famine. They'd stayed on and Mrs. Dinsmore taught in our village school. Unlike many teachers provided by the English, she never forced a student to wear a dunce cap for using an Irish word. Nor sent a child home for dirty feet after he'd walked miles to school.

Gran said a decade of the rosary every night for the Dinsmores to turn Catholic before it was too late.

After we crossed a small bridge, the road widened slightly. As we creaked open the gate to Saint Brigid's, Father Sheehy looked up from the rose hedge he was trimming. "I sent word by the fastest messenger I could," he said with an impish smile. He set the clippers on the low stone wall. "I'd have come myself, but I'd promised to pay a visit to Mrs. Feeney."

We followed the stooped, white-haired priest into the cool dark of a musty room. He drew out a chair. "Sit down, Nora. A letter's come addressed to me, but Delia's words are meant for you." My grandmother turned pale and her fingers tightened around the top of her cane. "It's not bad news, Nora. But it's too bad Delia didn't see fit to write you directly." He shook his head and sighed. "For some, old grudges die hard."

The phrase *old grudges die hard* gave me an uneasy feeling.

As my grandmother scanned the single sheet of paper; the lines around her mouth deepened. She glanced my way for no more than a second and my uneasiness grew. Then, biting her lip, she held the letter out to me, her hand trembling.

I read it three times and still couldn't believe what Delia had written.

CHAPTER 2

"I'm not going to America," I said, handing the letter to Father Sheehy."

"But it's a grand opportunity, Mary. Your aunt is offering a chance for a fine education," Father Sheehy replied;

Gran's knuckles had turned a mottled blue-white on the top of her cane. When she didn't speak, I blurted out, "I won't live with an aunt who has a heart of stone."

Gran gasped. "Where did you hear such a thing? Who said it?"

I had to look away from her grim expression. "Under the table when you left the room for a few minutes," I muttered. "It was long time ago and Mrs. Laughlin said it."

"The trouble maker, herself. I should have guessed." She covered her mouth as if to hold back a torrent of words.

Father Sheehy cleared his throat. He waited, glancing from me, then to Gran. "Nora, surely, you've told Mary about her mother's only sister." When she didn't answer, he turned to me. "After what you overheard, weren't you curious to learn more?"

"I was curious," I admitted.

"Why didn't you just ask your grandmother about what you heard?"

"I don't know….It seemed…" I couldn't go on because I really didn't know why.

He shook his head "You need to speak up, Mary Clarey." His expression was stern as he faced my grandmother. "No matter what happened between you and Delia, you should have told Mary her mother had an older sister."

"I did nothing wrong."

"Sometimes doing nothing is the greater sin."

To my grandmother, who struggled if she mistakenly ate a bit of meat on Friday, or arrived two minutes late for Mass, there was no worse accusation.

After an uncomfortable silence, Father Sheehy said more softly, "Delia's made a generous offer, Nora. Haven't you said yourself there's little on the west coast of Ireland to hold young people?" She didn't answer. He turned to me. "Twelve is a perfect age to be going on to a higher education. You're a fine scholar, Mary. Don't dismiss this offer lightly. Not many have such a grand opportunity."

I followed his glance to the map tacked up above a straight-backed chair. Smudged fingerprints traced the Atlantic crossings of sons and daughters who'd been leaving Ballydare since the potato blight over thirty years before when a fungus swept over Ireland, leaving blackened leaves, rotting potatoes and starvation. Many died from hunger, many from the fever that followed like a second plague. Now, news from Boston and New York held more interest than news from Dublin. A few children had come back to visit. None had stayed in Ballydare more than a few months.

As my grandmother stood silently, the old priest suggested, "Delia included a return address. This doesn't have to be decided today. You can write back in a few days."

"'Tis you she wrote to, Father. Delia wants no word from me."

"You don't know that, Nora."

"I know what I know." she said in a sharper tone than I thought she'd use with a priest.

He shrugged his shoulders, scanned the letter in his hand, then said, "Let's walk down to the store. You can talk this over with Pat and Aggie. Your son has a good head on his shoulders, and Aggie's a rock of common sense."

∞

Before I could read, I believed the sign above my uncle's store said "Pat and Aggie's," not Reardons, and thought they must be very important people to have so many people stopping by to talk. Today, the store was empty for a change.

As we pushed open the door to the usual jingling bell, smell of tea and smoked fish, Uncle Pat looked up from The Galway Times. My aunt smiled and continued separating brown eggs from white into reed baskets. After a brief greeting, Father Sheehy spoke in a low voice to Uncle Pat, who nodded and accompanied the priest outside.

Aunt Aggie raised her eyebrows. "Has Father brought news of trouble from Galway?"

"From America," Gran answered. "Delia wants Mary to live with her."

"Delia! Your Delia?" She laid two white eggs in a basket and pushed it aside. "Sure and she must be daft, expecting the child to go off to a stranger." Wiping her hands on her apron, she said, "Come have a cup of tea while Pat puts an end to such nonsense"

Encouraged by my aunt's reaction... Father Sheehy was right...My aunt and uncle were rocks of common sense... I followed her through the door that opened into a row of rooms behind the store. She settled Gran into the rocker, brought out three teacups, mumbling, "America, indeed. Daft!"

My grandmother and I waited silently until she returned with a pot of strong tea. She set a filled cup in front of Gran. Sinking heavily into a chair, Aunt Aggie said, "If there's to be any moving, you and Mary should come here." She looked straight at Gran. "You shouldn't spend another winter in that drafty house the way your rheumatism's been acting up."

My sense of relief sank slightly. Her words allowed a tiny crack, letting in change. "Gran and I do fine by ourselves," I protested. "I keep the turf fire going. Carry in the water when it's raw out."

"You do all that and more, Mary," Gran replied. "But isn't it lonely for you, so far from those your own age?"

"No. I go to school. I come into the village when we need something---."

Aunt Aggie broke in, "But you would be closer to those your own age living here." As four-year-old Lizzie climbed onto her lap, she placed a hand on her curly red hair. "I'd hate to see any one of my own go off to America. A terrible feeling it must be, never to see a child again."

Silence fell over the room. My mother, Gran's youngest child, had set out on a calm and sunny day. Neither she nor my father was seen again after a squall swept over their small boat. Delia had gone to America, never to be seen again. I was even more determined not to leave my grandmother.

Aunt Aggie stirred her tea briskly. I sipped mine slowly. Why was it taking so long? All Uncle Pat had to say was, "Mary belongs here. Delia's no more than a stranger now."

The awkwardness didn't lift until my cousin, Jamesy, burst into the room. "Da says me and Maggie can pick berries at the Big House. Edmund's gone back, 'cause the Dinsmores promised to buy all he can get." He held out a pan. "Want to come with us, Mary?"

But I wanted to stay behind to hear how Uncle Pat convinced Father Sheehy Delia's letter was ridiculous. Before I could say I didn't want to pick berries, my uncle spoke from the doorway. "Run along with Jamesy and Maggie, Mary. We'll not be deciding anything today."

I looked toward my grandmother, remembering the time she had said no so sternly to my going to Ashmont. To my surprise, she nodded permission.

I followed Jamesy. Hoping that Father Sheehy wouldn't fill Uncle Pat's head with talk of grand opportunities, I comforted myself with the priest's words. "Your son has a good head on his shoulders and Aggie's a rock of common sense."

But my uncle's words, "We'll not be deciding anything today." bothered me.

Shouldn't that decision be mine?

CHAPTER 3

Reluctantly, I trailed my cousins up a scrubby hill, then into a grove of oak trees. As we pushed through a mass of rhododendrons, I caught my breath!

The house and what remained of the gardens of Ashmont could fill the village of Ballydare. Blocks of gray stone rose four stories high. Narrow windows stretched so tall, I could hardly imagine how high the ceilings must be, or how large the rooms. The house was not a castle, I knew from pictures of grander places, but it was close enough. Several statues lay toppled on the ground, but a stone girl stood on a pedestal, facing the sea, her feet and arms draped in brush and weeds tossed by the winds that swept in from the Atlantic.

Letting Maggie and Jamesy walk ahead, I looked toward the ocean at a string of misty-blue islands. A chill crept along my arms and shoulders. I'd never had such a long clear view. I waited for tears, wished for them, instead of the ache behind my eyes.

Somewhere between those islands and the rocky ledge below, my parents had drowned. For a second I almost believed the stone girl had watched as their little boat was tossed and toppled by wind and waves. Then as I rejected the foolish notion that a stone statue could see or feel, it was as if a patch of fog lifted. I remembered the morning I'd trailed after Gran asking question after question about my parents. How abruptly she'd gone outside and stared at the ocean. When I followed, she'd smiled, and said she was counting the fishing curraghs. But I knew she was just pretending. My questions had made her sad. From then on, I waited until she chose to talk about my mother or my father, and cherished every scrap of information she gave.

Over time, I learned my father, James Cleary, was twenty-two years old when he set out with turf for one of the islands, which had no bogs, so no fuel of its own. My mother, seventeen, had gone along to visit a friend who'd married an island boy. I'd stayed behind because I had a touch of colic. My grandmother often ended her brief bits of information with the comment, "Mary Ellen wasn't meant for this world."

I was left to wonder. Had my mother been too good for this world? Or had this world not been a good enough place for her? It was a troubling thought. I knew I was in no danger of being too good for this world, but I never did give my grandmother any unkind words.

My memories were interrupted when Maggie called, "Edmund said the berries are so ripe they're falling into the pans." I ran to catch up. Jamesy had pulled apart the web of ivy growing over a long window of the Big House. The three of us peered into a room that could easily have held Gran's entire cottage. Dappled light fell on furniture covered by sheets. A ray of sun glinted off a gold-framed painting of a man and woman with forbidding faces.

Maggie drew her arms tight across her chest. "Don't they look English, Mary?"

Jamesy whispered, "Matt Harrigan's father says their ghosts come back from England to haunt this place. He saw them when he came up looking for his strayed cow."

I laughed. "Jamesy, you know Matt's father collects the rents for those ghosts in England. He says that so people won't come up and steal anything."

"Being a rent collector doesn't mean he couldn't have seen ghosts," Jamesy said as if that settled the matter.

"They'd be chasing us with sticks if they caught us taking their berries," Maggie whispered

"They're *our* berries," Jamesy snapped. "Mam's grandfather planted them. Besides, they'll fall off and be squished if we don't pick them."

We walked on toward the berries which really were ripe enough to fall into our pails. I distanced myself from their chatter to prepare myself. Whatever reasons anyone gave for going to America, I'd better start thinking of better reasons to stay.

In a few minutes Edmund Burke picked his way to the canes I was stripping. "I tried to hail you on your way to the village, Mary. Your gran must have been in a hurry, not stopping to rest."

"Father Sheehy sent for us. He had a letter from an aunt I don't even know. She wants me to come live with her in America."

"America!" He brushed berry stained fingers through his wavy red hair. "Some people have all the luck. When are you going?"

"I'm not going." I leaned into the canes, and snatched at a clump of berries. Why should I be off to live with a stranger? Everything I want is here."

"Then you can't be wanting much, Mary." He sighed and looked at the ground. "Mam and I talk all the time about America. Someday I'll scrape up the money and we'll go there."

As he stretched deep into the brambles, I continued along the outside canes, trying to picture Edmund and his mother away from Ballydare.

"Poor Mae Burke" most of the village called her, the way she wandered about, looking for her mother or father, or her little sister, all dead years ago in the famine. Edmund's father had gone to America to work on the roads, and been killed in an accident before he could send for his wife and year-old son.

Now, Edmund, the brightest boy in school, stayed home days at a time to look after his mother. Once, my uncle said, "Poor Edmund Burke," and I'd blurted out, "Don't call him that. It's unlucky." Uncle Pat never said it again.

When our pans were full, we stopped in front of the Big House for a last look. "Can you imagine living in such a grand place, Mary?" Maggie asked. "You'd have to cut tons and tons of turf to keep warm."

"They didn't cut their own turf, Eejit." Jamesy sounded as bitter as the old men who'd lived through the famine. "They kept us Irish working for pennies, so's they could be living the life of lords and ladies."

"Well, Mam says the Ashtons weren't as bad as some. They never pressed for the rent in the bad years. They sent down food to the---"

"It was our land, and they stole it."

"You mustn't be so full of hate, Jamesy. Father Sheehy says…"

Edmund and I left the bickering and walked over to the statue. He pulled the tangled brush from the stone girl's outstretched arms, revealing a basket of apples. "Don't you think she would be offering those apples to the people in the house?" I asked.

"Maybe she's Irish and doesn't want to look at the fine English house."

"You sound like Jamesy. Do you hate the English?"

Edmund looked at me with a wry smile. "I'm Father Sheehy's altar boy. I'm not supposed to hate anyone. But I understand the people who do."

He shrugged and walked away to where the land dropped off. After half a minute he called, "Come look, Mary. From up here the story stone looks like a big potato." When I joined him he pointed to the winding road below. "Remember how I'd tag along to hear your gran's stories of the wee people who ruled their little kingdoms between the stone walls?"

I laughed. "The Wee Feeneys against The Tiny Tunneys. They took turns outsmarting each other, nobody was ever hurt, and only those with a special gift could see them."

"Your Gran never would say if she had seen them or not." Edmund shook his head. "At first I thought every tale was true. I'm glad she told us the funny stories first."

We fell silent. For miles and miles, a crazy quilt of greens and tans and yellow seamed with stone walls told the true story. It was not The Wee Feeneys and Tiny Tunneys who ruled the land below. It was the English.

Gran's little rock-bound kingdoms were fields, divided so often that families had barely

enough land to plant potatoes, a few vegetables, and raise a cow for themselves. A half-chimney marked where the Coynes had died in the famine of 1845. The field of yellow furze once held the Ryan's' ponies. The Ryans had died in 1848 of famine fever on the ferry to Liverpool.

Once, I'd heard Granda muttering when the rent collector passed by our cottage, "Thanks be to God, and my grandfather, the Reardons own their land, and are beholden to no one. Least of all the English."

When I'd asked how his family had been so lucky, he'd answered, "The Reardons bred and trained Connemara ponies, and my grandfather knew the cures for any ailing horse. He promised to work only with the Ashton horses and ponies in exchange for the title to this land. When the blight struck, we'd no fear of being tossed out on the roadside; our house tumbled, because we couldn't come up with the rent."

It was Edmund who broke the silence. He pointed to a ship on the horizon. "Off to America, it must be."

"Or Canada. Or Australia," I added. "I saw one earlier today." The smoke broke into smaller puffs, and I forced a laugh. "See, even the clouds don't want to leave Ireland."

"But the people on the ship do," Edmund said, still gazing out to sea. "And they'll be sending money back so's their brothers and sisters can follow, because America is such a grand place."

I didn't answer him. Jamesy and Maggie had already disappeared into the banks of rhododendrons and Edmund started after them, calling over his shoulder, "I'll miss you, Mary. But I still think you're lucky to be going."

"I'm *not* going. I'm *never* leaving here." I shouted after him.

I clutched the pan to my chest. Beyond the fields, the sea sparkled. Above the curraghs, gulls called out their claims to scraps. The air was sweet with wildflowers and the berries I was holding. I couldn't, I wouldn't leave Ireland. And no matter what was being discussed in my absence, I was not going to leave Gran. As long as I was here to help her, she and I could manage just fine.

When I caught up with my cousins, Edmund was already out of sight. Maggie and Jamesy had stopped quarreling, and were deciding how they'd spend the pennies their mother would give them for each jar of jam she sold.

Maggie and Jamesy took their berries out to the store. I sat opposite Gran who had fallen asleep with her rosary beads in her hands.

When Gran woke, she looked around as if to place where she was. Then she smiled. "Ah, Mary, you're back. Did you get a good lot of berries?"

"Enough for some pies, and a few jars of jam."

"That's nice." Then looking at me intently, she leaned forward and said the one thing I wasn't prepared for. "Sure, it's an answer to prayer, I've had, Mary. An answer to prayer."

As my grandmother drew in a deep breath, I held my own. What could possibly have happened, or been said, while I was at the Big House?

Gran's eyes never left mine. "All these years, I've been storming heaven for some great good to come into your life, Mary. I was half-way through my beads when I must have nodded off. I dreamed you were in a grand city, and I was reading your letters to all who'd listen."

She sat back and rocked gently. "I can't be denying you an education far beyond what you'd be getting here. Delia will make sure of it. A great reader she was, like you. Even as a child she'd be waiting for your Granda to finish his newspaper, to keep up with all that went on."

"You're only saying nice things about Delia so I'll want to go," I protested. "Delia's mean, Gran. She's never let you know how she is, or written to ask how you are."

My grandmother fingered her beads and took a deep breath. "Whatever went on between us, she won't hold against you, Mary. Delia is fair. She couldn't forgive what she saw as unfairness in others."

"But you and Granda were never unfair. She must have been the one who was wrong." I waited for some explanation of what had happened.

Gran rocked slowly without looking at me. Finally she said firmly, "I'll not be turning your mind against her by giving my side. You'll have changes enough in a new land without being saddled with troubles from the past."

I was close to tears. "But I don't want to leave you. I don't want anything to change."

She stopped rocking and leaned toward me. "Changes come whether we like it or not. Before you know it, you'll be a young woman, and I'll be changing, too. I'm feeling my years." She smiled as Lizzie, her youngest grandchild, climbed onto her lap. Laying her hand on Lizzie's head, she added, "Well, I'm not so old

I can't be a help with the new one. Even on my worst days, I can rock a cradle."

She must have seen the surprised look on my face. "You didn't know? If you haven't wondered why Aggie's filling out around the middle, you must still be thinking babies come out of the cabbage patch."

Embarrassed that I hadn't realized, I protested. "I know more than that. I heard Josie Norris and Mame Conley talking."

"Well, those brazen girls aren't the ones to be telling you about such matters." The bell jangled over the door to the store. Gran cocked her head as a customer ordered biscuits, then a slab of cheese. "We'll talk later. You're not going off to America unprepared for life, Mary."

At that moment I knew my grandmother's belief that her prayers had been answered could not be shaken. But from the little I knew of my aunt in America, Delia Reardon didn't seem a likely answer to prayer.

THEA GAMMANS

CHAPTER 4

For the next few weeks, since no one mentioned America, I dared to hope the trip might never come about. But on a Monday morning, we heard rattling, followed by neighing, then "Whoa, Boyo."

Father Sheehy pulled up to the gate. As he climbed down from his trap he called, "I thought Delia might write to you this time, Nora, but she had a few instructions for me."

Gran scowled at the letter in his hand. "Instructions for a priest, indeed,"

"She only suggested matters a parish priest can handle best." He patted his old horse on the rump, left it to munch on the grassy tufts along the roadside, and followed us into the house.

There was a loaf of freshly baked bread on the table and a dish of preserved berries. "No one makes finer soda bread, or brews a better pot of tea than you, Nora Reardon," he said as if he had dropped in for a friendly visit.

Gran smiled at the obvious flattery. I set out three plates, three cups and saucers, and a slab of butter, as she sliced half a dozen slices of bread. The letter remained in Father Sheehey's hand. While the tea steeped I waited anxiously, dreading what Delia might have written. Finally, Father Sheehy cleared his throat and began to read.

The enclosed sum should be more than adequate to

provide passage for two in second cabin. Mary must have a companion for the crossing, a healthy girl, at least sixteen years of age, with a pleasant nature and good character. According to her abilities, this girl will be given a position as household help, be paid a fair wage, and be able to attend Mass on Sunday.

He raised his eyes. "Twenty-five guineas is a princely sum, Nora. Few have left these parts in second cabin. Delia must be in very comfortable circumstances so Mary will not be wanting for anything."

"Nothing but a soft word now and then. It's not in Delia's nature." Gran muttered, almost as if she were talking to herself.

The priest looked back at the letter and cleared his throat again. "One more thing. Delia wants Mary and her companion to leave by the end of this month. There's a ship going out of Galway. Directly to Boston"

I gasped. "That's too soon!"

Gran said, "Surely, there's no great hurry---."

"Perhaps it's to take advantage of the weather, before the seas get rough." He folded the letter and slipped it into a pocket. He sipped his tea, eyes cast down as if he were lost in thought.

"That was lovely, Nora," he said at last, brushing crumbs from his fingers onto the plate. "Now, I'm thinking Theresa Noonan would be just the girl to go with Mary. She's a fine, strapping girl, and the family can use whatever bit of money she sends home."

Gran's eyes narrowed. "Is it the Noonans on the Folly Road you're speaking of, Father?"

The old priest chuckled. "I haven't heard that desolate stretch called the Folly Road in years. Yes, that's the family."

I barely knew the Noonans, but I did know the road. Going from nowhere to nowhere, the Folly Road had been laid down during the famine to provide work for men who were paid too little to feed one worker, let alone a family. Now only the poorest families lived there.

My grandmother frowned. "Tim Noonan's daughter? Sure, and he'd be spending every cent she sent back on drink."

"Tim's a good man when he's sober and he's never raised a rough hand to any of them. But I'll have a talk with Theresa about seeing the money gets to her mother." Father Sheehy stood up and stretched his shoulders. "A promising lad he was, with his quick wit and good looks. Every girl in the village hoped he'd look her way."

"And look at him now, a disgrace to his family, begging from house to house for money for drink," Gran said. "No daughter of his could be a fit companion for Mary."

"You mustn't judge the whole family by the father's weakness, Nora. Theresa is a good girl and a great help to her mother and I've been after Tim for years to take the pledge to stop drinking. Tomorrow, I'll say Mass for the Noonan family. They've a hard cross to bear."

Father Sheehy's prayers carried great weight with my grandmother, and she offered no more objections to having Theresa Noonan go to America with me.

But as we watched the old priest drive off, I still had plenty of objections to going to America. "Gran you need me here," I said as I followed my grandmother into the cottage. "Your knees ache if you walk to town in the rain. I've always been the one to carry in the water."

"Pat will see that I have anything I need and check that I have water in the house."

"It could be blowing hard, a sudden storm come. You couldn't chase the geese...."

But my words carried no weight at all. Gran wouldn't listen, and I knew that every day she would only grow more convinced that her prayers had been answered.

CHAPTER 5

When Aunt Aggie heard how soon I was to leave, she offered to make me some new dresses. Gran's rheumatism was bothering her, so I walked to town by myself to be fitted.

A heavy fog had settled along the shore road. The waves slapped against the rocks, the only evidence that the ocean was so close by. As I approached the story stone, I tried to picture myself beside my grandmother on a sunny day, with Gran thoroughly enjoying the tales she made up as Edmund clapped his hands when the Wee Feeneys did something truly clever. But it was no use. The trip to America blotted out happy memories as effectively as the fog hid the sea. I hurried faster toward the bustle and warmth of my aunt's house.

As soon as I arrived, Aunt Aggie hauled a dozen bolts of cloth from the back of the store into the house for better light. "Pick out what you like best, Mary," she said. "I'll run up some new dresses. We can't have you arriving shabby."

I touched blue-and-white checked gingham, and hesitated between a striped pattern and a design with sprigs of lavender flowers and green leaves. Aunt Aggie smiled at me over a length of white cotton she was measuring at arm's length. Her forehead was glistened, her round face beamed with pleasure, as if she were taking off on the trip herself. "You'll have all three. With a couple of pinafores, you'll be crossing in high style."

I felt a knot in the pit of my stomach. Was I leaving an aunt who was, as Gran put it, "all heart" to go to one with a heart of stone? .

I was standing on a chair when Aunt Aggie said through a mouthful of pins, "Stand straight, Mary, or I'll never get the hem right." I pulled myself from the slouch I'd fallen into when I discovered I was half a head above Bridget Murphy, who was a year older. "You'll soon grow into your height," Aggie said. "You take after your Gran. I'll leave a deep hem in case you grow another few inches."

I watched in horror as she left four inches, then fixed the waistline with another three inches that could be let down.

When she'd finished pinning, she stepped back. "That looks fine. You'll get at least two years before you have to let it down." Then she looked directly at me, smiled, and patted her stomach. "I'm in the family way, Mary. The baby is due before Christmas."

I blushed, realizing that Gran had told her I hadn't recognized why she'd grown so big around the middle.

Then with a smile, followed by another pat on her stomach, she added, "Mary, in a few years I'll be telling Maggie what I'm about to tell you. When a girl reaches a certain age, she will see some bleeding each month. It would be a. terrible fright if she hadn't been told ahead of time. But it means that she's old enough to have a baby."

"I know about the curse," I said, looking toward the floor.

"Curse is a terrible word for what's natural, Mary." My aunt shook her head. "Sometimes young girls exchange terrible tales, because their mothers haven't prepared them..." She fell silent for several seconds, and then laid her hand on my shoulder. "Your Gran would find it hard to talk to you about this. She'd be reminded of her loss, and thinking it's your own mother should be telling you what a girl needs to learn." She stood back again to inspect the evenness of the hem, then looked directly at me. "This isn't likely to come about for a few years, Mary. There's more to it, but I've told you enough for a girl your age. As long as you know there's men and boys alike who'd take advantage of a young girl's innocence. If anyone asks you to do something you'd be ashamed to tell the priest, wipe your hands of him. A man who takes advantage of a girl's innocence isn't worth the time of day."

I blushed again, remembering the snickers of Josie and Mame.

I was spared further embarrassment when the bell jingled. Uncle Pat called in from the store, "The Noonans have come to call. I'm sending them in to see you."

Mrs. Noonan was gaunt, with deep-set, haunted-looking eyes. The little boys by her side were scrubbed, but shabby, their bare feet dusty after the long walk from the Folly Road. They glanced around timidly. A few steps behind, a girl with a tangle of red hair partly hiding her face fingered the skirt of her faded dress. I knew her only as Theresa, a girl who had seldom made it to school and stopped coming at all a few years ago.

My aunt gestured toward empty chairs. "A few more pins and I'll have this hem in place. I've hardly seen you since we were in school together, Eilly. Theresa's grown so, I'd barely recognize her."

"She's seventeen," her mother said. "If there's children to be taken care of, she's had plenty of experience."

I would never have guessed that the worn frail woman was the same age as my aunt. But as Aunt Aggie reminisced about their days in school, Eilly Noonan's responses were bright and funny, and I could almost see what she must have been like before life on the Folly Road.

Theresa, on the other hand, perched on the edge of a chair and mumbled "yes" or "no" to questions. My aunt made several attempts to draw her out, then said to her mother, "I've been making a few outfits for Mary. I'd like to run one up for Theresa as a going-away present." She pointed to the bolts along the far wall. "Pick out the material you like best, Theresa." She turned to the boys, "Off with you to the store and tell Mr. Reardon I said you can each have a licorice stick."

The boys dashed out while Theresa gazed at the bolts like a child in front of a tray full of sweets. After a deep breath, she pointed to a roll of brilliant green. "I like this."

"Isn't that a bit bold?" her mother asked my aunt.

"With her red hair and green eyes it will be stunning." She smiled at Theresa. "You'll look simply grand at the party."

Eilly Noonan gasped. "There's to be a party?"

"A send-off for the girls. It won't be a wild affair." She glanced at the little boys and lowered her voice. "There'll be no alcohol served, Eilly."

I knew she was referring to the "American Wakes," filled with songs, fiddles, and laughter, along with tears and too much to drink because those leaving would probably never be seen again. Theresa lowered her head and stared at her worn shoes. I was glad Gran wasn't there to see the girl who was supposed to look after me.

I suspected I would be the one looking after Theresa.

CHAPTER 6

As I prepared for my trip, everyone spoke as if there were only wonderful things in my future. "A lovely name for a ship, "*Halcyon* is", Aggie said as she laid my finished dresses in the tapestry bag she'd made for the trip. Mr. Dinsmore, who was always filled with interesting facts, said he'd heard Galway was Columbus' last port as he sailed off to discover America

Although part of me welcomed these as cheerful comments, a larger part hung on to all the wonderful things I was leaving behind.

Then suddenly, it seemed, my final day in Ballydare arrived. As we set out in the trap for Pat and Aggie's with two baskets full of breads and preserves Gran had made for the party, Uncle Pat whistled as though this were any ordinary day. My grandmother said, as she had been saying since early morning, "I hope it doesn't rain."

"There's not a cloud in the sky," my uncle replied. "Perfect weather for a party."

Gran took my hand; as I stared at a boat on the horizon, so she wouldn't see that I was on the verge of tears. She held it tight until we drew up in front of the store.

Aggie was setting a butter-crock filled with wildflowers in the center of the boards my uncle had placed over barrels. After taking Gran's contributions, she stepped back to inspect the table with a critical eye. "Everything looks lovely. But if anyone offers Tim Noonan a swig of poteen, it will ruin the evening. It would be a shame to have Theresa's last night spoiled."

"I'll keep a close eye on him," Uncle Pat promised. He put his hand on my shoulder. "It's low tide. I'm taking the children to gather sea moss. You come, too, Mary."

Uncle Pat seldom gave a direct order. I knew I was being told to come for a reason.

Maggie and Jamesy ran ahead. I walked along beside my uncle and Lizzie. The late afternoon sun cast a glow and I gazed at each house we passed as if I were seeing it for the last time. When we reached the shore my uncle told Lizzie, "Gather moss with your brother and sister while Mary and I talk a bit." He brushed seaweed from the skeleton of a wrecked boat. "We'll sit here and watch." he said as the children scrambled around the rocks for the moss Aggie used to make her puddings set. After a few minutes he turned and faced me. "I know you must be wondering about your Aunt Delia, Mary."

I nodded and waited, not knowing what to say.

He clasped his hands and leaned forward, looking down at the gray sand. "I was no more than a boy when Delia left. I'd been off for a few days, cutting turf with my cousins, and when I came back, my sister was throwing her things into a cloth bag. My father stared into the fire. My mother, pale as a ghost, had turned her back to Delia.

"Hello and Goodbye to you, Pat." Delia shot at me. "You'll not be seeing me after today." Uncle Pat took a pinch of tobacco from a pouch and tamped it into his pipe.

"Didn't she tell anyone why she was angry, not even later in a letter?"

"Not so much as word. Never an address where she could be reached or I'd have written to her."

He raised his eyes. "She was barely to the gate when the baby, Mary Ellen, who was to grow up to be your mother, took after her, wailing, 'Deliee...Deliee', like her little heart would break. Delia turned only the once." He paused as if to gather his words then continued. "Sure, I never saw such a tragic look as was on my sister's face at that moment. Then she flew off, too fast for the child's legs to catch up. I had to scoop Mary Ellen into my arms and haul her into the house. For days, the poor wee thing kept asking, 'Where's Delie? Where's my Delie?' For weeks, she ran to the door at the sound of a footstep on the path."

My uncle stopped to light his pipe. I stirred the rough sand with my foot, making swirling patterns in the gravelly sand. While my cousins laughed and splashed through the pools left by the ebbing tide, my tears welled up but didn't spill over as I pictured a broken hearted baby, chasing after the big sister she would never see again. I had never thought of my mother being so young before.

When the pipe was drawing to his satisfaction, Uncle Pat continued. "I never knew what the row was about. My mother refuses to discuss it. For the life of me I can't fathom what could have caused such a rift."

"Well, it *had* to be Delia's fault," I protested. "Gran never says a harsh word to anyone."

"Not in your memory, maybe. She could scold with the best of them if she had a mind to when we were children."

"But she was never unfair."

He drew on his pipe, as if he had to consider a moment. "Mostly, we got what was coming to us." Then he added with a smile, "She's mellowed with age."

As my uncle continued to draw on his pipe, I watched my cousins dash about, yanking purple-black moss from the dark stones. A slight breeze stirred when the tide turned. With the water's edge inching forward, Maggie moved quickly from stone to stone. Jamesy stayed beside the biggest rock which he had claimed as his own. Lizzie ran helter-skelter, grabbing fistfuls of wet moss from the lowest stones.

When the lapping waves filled the shallow pools, we started back. My older cousins carried the sacks of moss, Uncle Pat carried Lizzie. I walked beside him, still seeing the baby running after her big sister.

Was my aunt sending for me because she couldn't forget Mary Ellen, the baby who had loved her so? If so, I was not only sorry to be going off to a strange land, but worried. I wasn't the loving child she remembered. The perfect child Gran could barely bring herself to talk about.

Would I be a disappointment?"

When we heard a single pipe playing in the distance, Uncle Pat shifted Lizzie and placed his free hand on my shoulder.

"You're a grand girl, Mary. Delia will be proud of you. Maybe, when you've been there a bit, you can get her to write. It would mean a lot to your Gran."

"I'll try," I promised.

I felt better as we continued to the party I knew was gathering around Reardon's Store. A letter from Delia would mean a lot to Gran and Uncle Pat. If my aunt had any heart at all... if I talked about how kind Uncle Pat, her only brother, could be... if I reminded her of the wonderful stories Gran told about the Wee Feeneys and the tiny Tunneys... she would have to write.

∞

We rounded the bend, and the single pipe was joined by half a dozen fiddles. The crowd clapped. Several waved American flags. A Good Luck banner covered the Reardons' sign.

As I clutched my uncle's hand he squeezed it gently. "You could be the Queen, herself, the send off you're getting."

But I did not feel like a queen. And surely not Queen Victoria, whose very name made me think of the poor prisoners who'd been shipped off for stealing a bit of bread for their hungry families, or speaking their minds about ridding their country of the English.

Gran sat in the rocker in front of the store. Aggie, enormous in her Sunday dress, stood next to her. How had I not realized she'd be having a baby? She and several others in the crowd, now that I knew the obvious sign.

As more families arrived, the long tables over-flowed with brown breads, cakes, and biscuits. A large cold spiced beef in the center of one table, in a year the crops were not doing well, I suspected was a generous offering from Aggie's brother, who had a butcher shop in Galway.

When the fiddles began a jig, Pat said, "Run and join in the dancing, Mary."

Afraid I'd be all legs and elbows dancing, I shook my head and sat on an upturned nail keg next to Gran. The music was lively yet it filled me with the sad-sweet feeling that came when I smelled the first dry leaves of autumn. As Edmund Burke walked toward us with a smile, I thought how he had that same sweet sadness about him.

Edmund thrust a stone into my hand. "Tisn't much of a present, Mary, but you'd think it was a potato if you weren't holding it. The ring around the middle is supposed to mean it's lucky."

"I'll keep it always." I blushed and so did he.

"Will you write sometime, Mary? Tell me if America's as grand as they say?"

"If you promise to write back."

Gran spoke up then. "With postage so dear, you can slip a few sheets in with mine now and then, Edmund." He thanked her, blushed again, and went to the table filled with food. "The lad would be hard put to find the money for a stamp," she said shaking her head. "He's his mother's only blessing, poor woman."

Over the next hours, I was given half a dozen pouches of earth, at least ten dried shamrocks and as many live ones already beginning to wilt, along with several bits of peat wrapped in scraps of cloth. Hannah Laughlin had knitted a lovely white shawl for me, making me ashamed that I'd thought of her as only a nosy old gossip. Father Sheehy presented me with a book about the saints of Ireland, and said he knew I would represent all that was best in Irish womanhood in whatever I chose to be my vocation. Particularly teaching. The Dinsmores had sent a gift and a note saying they were sorry they could not be at the party. Mr. Dinsmore had fallen and was unable to leave his bed.

I hesitated. Was I supposed to open the wrapped gift? Gran nodded. It was a box of the loveliest writing paper I had ever seen, with a note asking me to send the occasional letter.

A hush fell over the crowd when the Noonans arrived. The children looked as if they'd been scrubbed within an inch of their lives with a bar of lye soap. But it was Theresa everyone stared at. The green dress gave her a figure nobody could have known she had. Her red hair was brushed back and gleaming. The young men stood with open mouths. The surprised girls were tight lipped, as if they were glad Theresa Noonan was leaving Ballydare in the morning.

Aunt Aggie took Theresa by the hand and twirled her around. "I knew that bolt of green was meant for someone striking enough to carry it off."

"Theresa's shoes are from the Dinsmores," Gran whispered. "They asked what would be most needed, and had the shoes delivered straight to the Noonans. Just like them to think of that."

"Yes, it is," I agreed, sorry I wouldn't have a chance to say goodbye to the Dinsmores.

As the evening wore on, men who hadn't taken the pledge slipped outside. Father Sheehy collared Tim Noonan as he eased toward the door. "You wouldn't want to be missing the prayers for your daughter's safe trip, would you?" he said wedging Tim between two pledge takers, who'd promised to see he didn't touch a drop.

After the families with young children left, the older women talked about how well their children and grandchildren in America were doing. A dozen men argued about the best way to get rid of the English once and for all, no three of them in agreement. Gran dozed in her chair.

By the time Uncle Pat drove us home, I was holding so many pieces of Ireland, I felt as if I'd been armed to do battle in a strange land.

I'd write to Gran first. Next, to Uncle Pat and Aunt Aggie, then to the Dinsmores. No matter what I thought about my aunt Delia, I'd find something good to say about her. When I had really made my mind up about America, I'd write to Edmund.

Tired as she was, Gran threw a block of turf on the fire to boil water. As we sipped our tea, she gave me the last gift.

"But it's your most treasured possession," I protested as she handed me the amber rosary beads her grandmother had received from an uncle who'd been a hedge priest, who'd hidden in the groves and ditches to say Mass, like the hedge teachers did in order to teach children to read and write when the penal laws were in effect.

"I've my every-day beads, and you'd be getting these sooner or later. They've been passed to the oldest daughter for three generations," my grandmother said.

I did not comment that I was not the oldest daughter, only the oldest granddaughter.

"I'll pray a decade for you every day, Gran, and I'll write every week," I said. The hearth fire and the oil lamp cast both light and shadows that made my grandmother's face seem softer and older. "And Christmas Eve, I'll set a lighted candle in a window facing the ocean like we always do," I added

"I'll come out here with Pat and light one myself," Gran promised.

That night, fingering the first ten beads on the rosary Gran had given me, I asked that I have a safe crossing, hastily adding Theresa Noonan so as not to seem selfish. On the second decade, I asked that I would someday return to Ireland. On the third, that Gran would live to a ripe old age so I would see her again. For the fourth, that all the people who attended the farewell party- I refused to call it "an Irish Wake"- would be blessed, including the Dinsmores who couldn't come. On the last ten beads, I asked that I could keep my promise to Uncle Pat and get Delia to write to Gran.

My mind was so full I couldn't fall asleep. I tossed and turned, then tried to lie still, listening to the waves splash against the shore. As I thought of the vast distance the ocean put between families, I wondered if the separation between Gran and Delia was as great. What deed could be so bad that it couldn't be forgiven? Would I be able to get either of them to write? Finally, I turned over and closed my eyes. Whatever happened, I was prepared for one thing.

In the waist of my blue flowered dress, in the space Aggie left in case I kept growing, I had tucked away the nine guineas left over from the twenty-five she'd sent for our passage.

If I was a disappointment and nothing like my mother, if my aunt didn't like me, and if Delia Reardon had the heart of stone I'd heard about, I had my fare home.

CHAPTER 7

My uncle, Theresa and I waited on the dock, surrounded by vendors chanting. "Last chance before America. Buy a sweet. A pretty ribbon. Limes for the crossing. Last chance before America." I drew in a sharp breath. Last chance! There was no turning back.

Uncle Pat shifted our bundles over his shoulder and took my hand. I pretended a cough. "It's the smell of tar bothering me." He squeezed my hand and I knew he wasn't fooled by my coughing.

The small boat that was to take us to the *Halcyon* had returned to the dock. A booming voice announced, "Second cabin passengers next." We made our way past jostling young men, and two mothers with oddly shaped bundles, cautioning children to stay close. My uncle passed our bags into the tender and wiped his forehead with his red kerchief. "Wave your kerchief until we're out of sight," I said to him, fighting tears. "I'll wave back."

With a choke in his voice, he answered, "Write as soon as you land, Mary."

He turned to Theresa, who hadn't spoken for over an hour. "You write home, too. Your mother will be anxious to hear from you." Theresa nodded and turned her head away.

We rode through the choppy water without speaking. As soon as we were on board the ship, Theresa asked one of the crew how to find our quarters in second cabin. I ran to the rail and stayed pressed against the wooden rail as the anchor was raised, waving and shouting, "Goodbye, Goodbye," to the red kerchief on the dock. Suddenly The Halcyon shuddered and sent up a huge belch of black smoke. With the wind cooling my cheeks as we moved forward, I watched Galway City grow smaller. When only a steeple remained in view, I continued to wave as if it would be disloyal to Uncle Pat if I stopped a moment sooner than necessary.

The distant hills took on a soft blue-gray. As we passed close enough to an island to see cottages and cows in a field, I waved for the last time and whispered, "Goodbye, Ireland."

When I couldn't tell whether the band of gray on the horizon was land or clouds, I picked up the two burlap bags Aggie had made for me and asked the same deck hand the way to second cabin. He pointed down a steep flight of stairs.

Our quarters were tight, but big enough for the ten days we expected to be on board. Theresa was sniffling on her bunk, an arm thrown across her eyes.

"Don't feel bad, Theresa," I said. "You'll soon be writing what a grand city Boston is, and sending back a few dollars."

"My poor mother," she wailed. "Not a soul to help her now. And little Mikey, he'll be missing me day and night."

Reminded that my own mother had run in tears after her big sister, I offered no easy words of comfort. Instead I took my new white shawl from the larger bag I shook it out. "When you feel better, come up on deck," I said, wrapping the shawl around my shoulders.

As I walked in the welcome fresh air, two children followed me, asking questions about everything on board. A white-haired woman called over, "Don't be wearing your sister out with questions." She beckoned us to come closer. "This is my seventh crossing. If I can't tell you what you want to know, you can ask one of the sailors."

"Seven times you've crossed!" I said in astonishment.

She smiled and rearranged the ball of cream colored yarn and the strip of knitting on her ample lap. "Not many but the sailors can make that statement." She invited us to sit down. We arranged ourselves at her feet, she asked our names and introduced herself as Mrs. Moriarty from Moyard, on her way to a son in Boston, then on to a daughter in Hartford. As she shifted into a comfortable position, I knew she was a woman who loved to talk.

"They both try to get me to stay in America," she began. "But then it's a letter from Ireland, and I'm on my way home again. I've children on both sides and can't be playing favorites, so I stay on the move, to keep in touch with the family. That's the important thing, keeping in touch. There's just so much you can put in a letter. " She stopped to count stitches, and then asked, "Is it to an older brother or sister that you children are going?"

"We're not together," I replied. "I'm going to my aunt."

"And is she in service in Boston?"

I hesitated. How could I explain I knew almost nothing about my aunt? The boy broke in. "Us Kelleys will be staying with our Uncle Matt. He's made heaps of money laying bricks."

The woman nodded approvingly. "My oldest boy, Petey, sent for his sister as soon as he had a few dollars ahead. Now he's done so well, the name P.J. Moriarty is known all over Boston. It's his generosity lets me travel on these grand, comfortable steamships. A far cry they are from the sailing ship, a regular coffin ship it was, that he took back in '49."

We sat hugging our knees as Mrs. Moriarty's voice rose and fell. We could almost hear the creak of Petey's vessel, see the passengers in little more than rags, taste the sour drinking water from kegs that once held vinegar. She kept our attention as well as the shanachees, story tellers who went from village to village with their tales of heroes and saints and mysterious happenings.

When a game of hide and seek started, Mrs. Moriarty said, "You shouldn't be listening to an old woman ramble on. Run and see the ship." As I left reluctantly, she called after us, "Stay on deck as much as possible to avoid the seasickness. Fill your lungs with fresh air."

I went below to tell Theresa about the woman who'd crossed seven times, hoping to cheer her up. The trip couldn't be that hard if Mrs. Moriarty kept going back and forth. But Theresa had her head to the wall and didn't answer when I spoke to her. Pretending to be asleep, I suspected. I left the cabin, annoyed. Wasn't I leaving my family, too? Going to a land I'd never seen. I doubted Theresa gave me a thought.

I went back to the rail. The gulls had deserted us. The ocean stretched ahead, vast and empty of everything but endless waves. I felt a great sweep of, not so much loneliness, but aloneness, something I had never felt before.

Our first meal was soggy potatoes and cabbage, and stringy boiled beef. But at least we wouldn't be on board for a month like Petey Moriarty. With good weather, steamships sometime made the crossing in as little as ten days.

After eating everything on her plate, Theresa felt seasick. I spent the remaining hours of daylight on the deck, picturing the village, then Gran, in the rocker beside Pat and Aggie's hearth telling Lizzie and Jamesy and Maggie about the little men with their rockbound kingdoms. I quickly replaced this picture with one of Gran in the store, sorting brown eggs from white, and setting aside those with cracks for baking.

By the time the sun had slipped behind a band of red-gold clouds, I had a plan. I'd tell my aunt about Mrs. Moriarty, an old lady, who had crossed the ocean seven times because she knew how important it was for a family to keep in touch when they lived far apart. Then I'd write to Gran and tell her the same thing. One of them would surely give in.

Convinced Father Sheehy would be proud of me, I went below. Theresa was asleep. I undressed, lay down on the narrow cot, and lulled by the hum of the engines, slept soundly through the night.

CHAPTER 8

"Come on deck with me Theresa," I pleaded after a breakfast of bread and tea.

"The sight of waves would turn my stomach for sure."

"Well, you can loll about feeling sicker and sicker down here, but not me," I said and left.

From the rail I watched the children stretch a rope from end to end. After each set of jumps it was raised a few inches higher. With my long legs, I knew I could easily leap over it, and joined in. When I was the last girl standing, I left the few gangly boys still jumping and settled down at Mrs. Moriarty's feet.

"Is that a gift you're knitting?' I asked.

She held out a narrow strip as if she were examining the size and shape of a finished product. "I've completed a fisherman's sweater on every trip. It's intricate enough to fill the hours, and I have something to give as a present."

We sat and talked in the warm sunshine and fresh breeze until the mid-day meal.

Soggy boiled potatoes again. Fish that hadn't been soaked long enough to remove most of the salt. Theresa ate, still complaining of seasickness. But I was not going to let her low spirits ruin the day and left.

As I walked along the deck, I pictured Gran opening a letter. She was brushing a tear from her cheek as she sat at the table to write back to Delia, when I heard a fiddle. A moment later a clear tenor voice was singing Rosein Dubh,…The Black Rose…a song that wasn't about a rose, at all, but was really about Ireland.

Since it never failed to bring a tear to every eye, and would give Theresa something different to cry about, I raced to the cabin. "Come quick," I called in. "There's a grand singer and you shouldn't miss him, Theresa." When she didn't respond, I added, "You'll be pale as a ghost by the time we land if you don't get a bit of sunshine."

"I suppose." She rose and draped a shabby gray shawl over her shoulders as if she expected to meet gale force winds.

We arrived on the very last line and had a clear view of the singer. Theresa clutched my arm. "Glory to God, Mary. You let me come up here looking like this." She turned and elbowed her way back through the crowd. I stood there, knowing exactly what she was going to do.

With his black wavy hair blowing in the breeze, and a face like one of the statues in a history book had suddenly smiled, the tenor asked if there were any requests. He had finished three songs when Theresa returned wearing her green dress, her red hair brushed, and her face scrubbed to a glow.

As he asked, "Will all the girls named Mary raise a hand," at least a third of the girls responded, having Mary somewhere in their name. My right hand was barely to my shoulder and Theresa lifted it higher. Of course, he couldn't help noticing Theresa, standing beside me. He never took his eyes off her as he sang.

"It wasn't her beauty alone that won me…
But Ah, t'was the truth in her eyes ever shining …
That made me love Mary, "The Rose of Tralee."

"Did you notice he was looking at you the longest?" Theresa said when the song was over.

"He was gawking at *you*," I replied.

She shook her hair and straightened her shoulders. "Do you really think so?"

"He stared straight at *you* when he sang 'twas not her beauty alone that won me." She blushed, and I added "You do look nice in that dress and when you fix your hair, Theresa."

The fiddler scraped a few notes and called out, "Tom Kerrigan will take one last request." Coins clattered from the deck above, where the railing was lined with first class passengers.

"Tom his name is," Theresa whispered. "Isn't that a grand name, Mary?"

Before I could reply, Tom doffed an imaginary hat to the upper deck, and pointed to a bunch of young boys, telling them to keep any coins they picked up. "And now for you rich Americans on your way home," he called with a wide smile, "my last song is about freedom, a cause dear to American and Irish alike. I want everyone to chime in on the chorus."

It was the strangest song I'd ever heard. I struggled with the images. The Lord who was loosing lightening...with a terrible swift sword...Trampling out grapes of wrath. Around me brows were furrowed. On the deck above, the passengers stood erect, almost at attention. But by the time the lines, *He died to make men holy let us die to make men free,"* all on board were caught up in the American song, and the Irish passengers joined the chorus in *Glory, glory, Hallelujah.*

As the crowd dispersed, Theresa announced, "I....I'll just stroll about a bit."

Mrs. Moriarty had set her knitting aside to join the audience. "A real crowd pleaser, he is, learning an American song before he's set foot in the country. He had everyone thinking they were Americans already." She picked up what was now clearly going to be a sweater. "I wouldn't be surprised to find the name Tom Kerrigan put up for city council in five years."

Although she spent only part of her time in Boston, Mrs. Moriarty knew all about wards and the places where the Irish vote was strong. As we talked she told me that although it took five years for an Irishman to become a citizen, the Irish were changing local politics, I listened with interest, but kept glancing around for Theresa. When she passed us arm in arm with Tom Kerrigan, I thought again of the girl who'd barely said a word as Aggie fitted her dress, and only a few days ago had spoken only to complain.

That night as we lay in bed, I thought she'd never stop talking. She turned a lime over and over in her hand, gazing at it as if it were an emerald. "When Tom gave it to me--for the seasickness, you know-- he said it not only matched my dress, it matched the color of my eyes. Can you imagine that, Mary? Tom noticing my eyes right off." She didn't wait for a response. I doubted she'd have heard one if I'd answered. "Tom's eyes change with what he's looking at. Sort of greenish they are, picking up the color of my dress. But looking at the sky, they're more blue. If it's cloudy they turn... "

Gray, I said to myself. I had never known anyone to go so completely daft as Theresa Noonan. Burying my head under the blanket, I began the rosary. The first decade of the beads I prayed for Gran as I had promised. The second ten beads were for Pat and Aggie and all their children including the one soon to be born. On the third set, I always prayed that the English would get out of Ireland. I hesitated on the fourth. Should it be for a safe passage, or peace between Gran and Delia? Peace, I decided. I'd have to have a safe trip for that. The fifth set of Hail Marys I usually left open, in case I got inspired to pray for some great need in the world.

As Theresa rambled on that no man or boy in Ballydare was a match for Tom Kerrigan, I found myself thinking of Edmund Burke. Not that he was like Tom. Edmund was shy and sang off key in school. But since he'd come so readily to mind, I said the fifth decade for him and his mother, and decided he'd be the first person outside my family I would write to.

∞

Theresa bounded out of bed cheerfully, and spent all day on deck in the company of Tom Kerrigan. We were only together for the tiresome boiled meats and overcooked vegetables. On the fourth night, with beet and cabbage juices flowing into the gray chunks of juices of mutton. I was glad an apple came with the meal.

Theresa carefully pared her apple skin into one long unbroken strip. Then with her eyes closed she tossed the peel over her shoulder.

"Doesn't that look like a T, Mary?" she asked. Though I didn't see any T, I agreed. She tossed the skin again. The peel resembled no letter at all. When the next toss vaguely resembled a K, she was convinced she had been shown the initials of the man she would marry.

I'd watched twelve and thirteen year olds girls do the same

with apples, even potato peelings, giggling and treating it as a game. But Theresa ate her apple dreamy eyed, as if she'd received a glimpse into the future. I felt like saying, "Silly Goose," but didn't have the heart.

∞

Four days later Mrs. Moriarty commented, "Tom and Theresa make a handsome couple, don't they?"

"She talks of no one else. It's Tom says, 'Don't the sparks from the stacks shoot out like stars in the night, Theresa? Put my coat around your shoulders to keep off the cold, Theresa?'"

"My Mary Frances was just as smitten, but it didn't last beyond the one summer." The old lady sighed. "I've often wondered how the shipboard romances I've seen turned out. People talk to strangers as if they've known them all their life. Maybe it's knowing they'll not meet again that they feel so free." She looked at Theresa and Tom standing at the rail. "I hope she doesn't have her heart broken. He's a lad who could charm the birds from the trees. It's good she's going with you, to a safe..."

She was interrupted by a succession of blasts from the ship's horn. As passengers and crew cheered, she laid her hand on my arm. "That's the signal we're halfway across. We've made good time. Run off and join the celebrating. When you come back, I'll have a treat for the occasion."

A crowd gathered in the bow, as if they could get that much closer to their destination. The Kelley children pressed against the rail, their hands shielding their eyes, as if they expected the shores of America any minute.

As the fiddle played I watched Theresa and Tom whirl about, amazed at how much she had changed in such a short time. Maybe there was hope for me. If she could go from being a timid girl, someday I might stop fearing I'd trip over my feet.

Mrs. Moriarty had spread a napkin across her lap and was slicing into a large, long fruitcake. "I saved this till the halfway point," she said as she handed thin moist slices to the Kelley children. "By the time we see land there won't be a crumb left."

Two women joined us, and the conversation turned to America and the future. But when the women left and Mrs. Moriarty packed up her knitting, and squinted at a narrow, dark line stretched across the western horizon.

"I don't like the looks of those clouds, Mary," she warned. "Don't eat heavily, and make sure you place anything you value under your mattress. There could be a lot of tossing about tonight."

CHAPTER 9

That night, as Theresa and I stripped down to our shifts, the *Halcyon* started to pitch and roll. At the shouts, "All lanterns out…all lanterns out," I doused the lamp.

We perched on the edges of our berths listening to the creaks and groans, as if wood and metal were being stretched to their limits. Through the thin partition we heard the muffled moans and cries of other passengers.

Suddenly there was such a lurch I thought the boat was about to break in half. I hid under the covers, pulled the flat musty pillow over my ears, and clutched my beads. A terrible fear swept over me.

The treacherous sea had claimed the lives of my mother and father. How could I ever have been lulled to sleep by the sound of waves lapping the shore? I began to shake, and must have cried out without knowing it.

Theresa came to the side of my bed and patted my back. "It'll be all right, Mary. It'll be over soon." With my stomach in knots, I leaned over the basin she held out to me. Nothing came up. I lay back down, shivering. Every shudder and roll of the vessel brought to mind the pitching and tossing little curragh on which my parents had set off to the islands

Eventually, I must have slept. I remember sitting up, sick at last, and Theresa saying, "Suck on this lime, Mary. It'll take the awful taste away." The sharp juice puckered my mouth, but it did calm my insides. I lay back, thinking how much nicer Theresa was to me than I'd been to her when she'd felt sick.

∞

It was afternoon before I went on deck. The storm had swept away every cloud. Crests of waves sparkled as if the night before had never been. Still queasy, I stayed back from the rail and watched a few pale children as they played quietly. Mrs. Moriarity came to her usual spot. "Wasn't that quite the tempest last night?" she called as she settled herself and began knitting what was now clearly a sweater. "Were you girls seasick?"

"I was." I picked up a ball of yarn which had fallen and sat down "I never knew a person could feel so sick…and frightened."

"And Theresa?"

"After all her complaining, she was the one calm and helpful."

As I rewound the woolen ball absently, Mrs. Moriarity commented, "You don't seem yourself, Mary. Is there more troubling you than the storm?"

Although I didn't mean to keep on, it all came spilling out. How with every pitch and toss of the ship, I'd realized how frightened my parents must have been.

"I never knew them," I sobbed. "I lived with my Gran and Granda 'til Granda died, then it was just Gran and me. Now I'm off to an aunt who's a stranger and has a heart of stone. She hasn't written so much as a note to Gran in years and years."

I was ashamed of the tears rolling down my cheeks, but couldn't stop. Soon I was telling Mrs. Moriarity about Delia's anger, my voice breaking as I described how my mother had run after her calling,"Delie, Delie". That I was afraid I would be nothing like the little girl Delia remembered. "She doesn't care for a soul in Ballydare," I said, sniffling and trying to dry my eyes. "Why should she care about me?"

Mrs. Moriarity reached into her bag and handed me a kerchief. "That was all before your time, Mary. Surely a grown woman wouldn't hold a grudge against a child." She rested the knitting on her ample lap and looked at me directly. "It could be that your aunt and your Grandmother are too much alike. Neither one admitting a wrong."

"Gran always apologizes if she's wrong."

"But your grandmother may believe she was in the right. Have you no idea what went on between them?"

I shook my head. "Even Uncle Pat doesn't know, and he was there when my aunt stormed out. But it couldn't be Gran's fault. It had to be Delia's."

Mrs. Moriarity was right about people on board ship talking to strangers. As we continued to talk her calm face and soft tone steadied me, and my fears subsided.

That night, since Theresa had been so thoughtful during the storm, I made a great effort to listen to every word as she rambled on and on about Tom. Finally I nodded off and slept soundly until morning.

CHAPTER 10

Despite the storm, the *Halcyon* was making good time. Passengers began placing bets on the hour we would arrive in Boston. The sun was high when Ned Kelley raced around calling "America. America! I see it."

"You're looking at Seal Cove, in Nova Scotia, Lad," a deck hand said. "From here on we'll not be out of sight of land for any length of time."

We crowded the rails, struggling to make out a barely visible shoreline. Contests started. Who would spot the next fishing boat? The next island? When two bigger boys shoved Ned in the ribs to make room for them, he and I left and sat next to Mrs. Moriarity

Shaking her head at the boys at the rail, who were now in a fist fight, she said, "They're Claddagh boys, I hear. There's a rough element in the Claddagh." She looked down to count stitches then added, almost sadly, " I hope there's someone on land to keep them in line, or they'll be joining the hoodlums who beat up newsboys and take away their good corners. It's their sort that give the Irish a bad name." She laid aside her needles and took a well wrapped fruitcake. She cut off three slivers of cake. "We'll save some for tomorrow after Mass."

It was the first I'd heard that the Irish had a bad name in Boston. None of the letters Gran had read aloud mentioned such a thing. But of course who would send back such news?

As we took tiny bites of the rich cake, to make it last, the old lady went on to explain. "There's country boys down from New Hampshire and Maine who go just as wild in the city, but I have to admit, there's too much fighting around the tenements and saloons in some Irish neighborhoods. Hardly a week goes by without someone from Ann Street or *Emerald Row* being hauled before the judge. It's a great source of embarrassment for the respectable Irish."

She picked up her needles again and pointed them at Ned. "Stay away from bad areas and keep out of fights. And if anyone tries telling you the Irish starved because they were too lazy to plant anything but potatoes, walk away. It's their own ignorance talking. Food was shipped from Ireland to England while the Irish starved."

Ned scowled, as if the last thing he'd ever do was walk away at such an insult. I'd heard the same words when Granda was alive, and old men gathered at the cottage to smoke their long clay pipes far into the night, planning ways to get the English out, plans they knew would never come to anything in their lifetimes.

"Take the pledge, Lad," she called after Ned as he left. "Make something of yourself. And stay away from places like Ann Street and Emerald Row." To me she said, "Take advantage of the opportunities ahead of you, Mary."

∞

When we gathered on the forward deck on Sunday for Mass, I was glad for the warmth of the white shawl around my shoulders. I'd covered my head with my new lace-edged kerchief. Theresa's gray shawl was draped over the back of her head, only the front of her red hair showing. There was a hush as the priest began. Seeing the distant smoke stacks of an eastbound ship, I wondered if the passengers were hearing the same Latin words. The same ringing of the little bell. It was comforting to think no matter how strange the new land might be, or even if we were in a jungle, or up among the Eskimos, the Mass would be the same.

A dozen or so people from first class joined us, whether because they had missed an earlier service, or because there was only one priest aboard, I didn't know. They were better dressed by far, and more confident, going up to talk with the priest when he'd finished. One portly, silver haired man walked through the crowd shaking hands. His prim little wife by his side nodded as if she were Queen Victoria herself.

Mrs. Moriarity nudged me. "That's Daniel O'Connor. Dandy O'Connor they call him. He's an important figure in South Boston. Shows up at every wake and funeral and never misses a chance to shake the hand of a future voter.

O'Connor was pumping Tom Kerrigan's hand even as Mrs. Moriarity spoke. When he placed a hand on Tom's shoulder, Tom glanced our way, then hurried toward us.

"Theresa," he said beaming. "The two of us... We've been invited up to first class to eat with the O'Connors tonight."

Theresa had pulled the shabby shawl off her head as soon as Mass was over. Now she fingered the knobby wool around her shoulders and glanced about as if she wanted to get rid of it.

"You'll be chilled without something over your shoulders," I said. "You can borrow mine." As we traded shawls, she looked so grateful, I felt I'd made up for the nights I'd buried my head under the pillow.

∞

That night, Theresa was glowing. "Elegant it was, Mary. Velvet and carpeting, and sparkling crystal... Like the Big House must have been when everything was polished and shining... And the ladies' dresses! I doubt they have the likes even in Dublin... The dinner was chicken in a creamy sauce, with the tiniest peas. I'll remember this day for the rest of my life."

After an hour, I ducked under the covers and pretended I was asleep.

CHAPTER 11

We awoke to a sea wrapped in fog. By afternoon the fog had lifted and from then on we watched for glimpses of blue-black islands with trees growing down to rocky ledges, or tiny harbors and clusters of wooden houses. Fishing boats, circled by hungry gulls, passed within hailing distance. What I'd always thought was the smell of the sea, I now realized was the earthy, salty blend where land and sea come together. At each deep breath, I felt anticipation coupled with uneasiness. I fingered the waistband of my dress. Before the dress was washed, I would remove the coins, and hide them in a safe place.

On our last night, I arranged the gifts I'd been given in a row on my cot. Wilted shamrocks, their leaves curled in upon themselves. Cloth pouches of crumbled soil. I touched Edmund's stone, hoping the ring of white really brought good luck. Like Theresa's memory of first class, I knew these moments would remain forever. I was no longer a girl who'd seen nothing beyond Ballydare except on a few trips to Galway city. I had crossed the Atlantic.

Excited and fearful in equal measure, I carefully folded the dress and placed it in the larger of my traveling bags. No matter what lay ahead, as long as I held onto those coins, I had my fare home.

CHAPTER 12

The *Halcyon* plowed past islands and lighthouses, boats of all sizes and descriptions, then entered Boston Harbor. Between arms of land, the city of Boston lay in a sunny haze. Gulls screeched what could be taken as a welcome or warning. Ned Kelley pointed to the highest spire. "We'll probably be meeting you there after Mass next Sunday, Mary."

"Maybe it's a protestant church," his sister said.

"Couldn't be," he scoffed. "Uncle Matt says half of Galway is in Boston. Us Catholics will be having the biggest church."

Mrs. Moriarity had promised to give me her address, saying she wanted to hear how things were going with me. I was still looking for her when the ship veered away from the long rows of docks ahead, toward a smaller row closer by. When I heard someone say, "We'll be taking a tender from East Boston" my heart skipped. Not another boat. Even for a short trip.

The first class passengers boarded the tenders before us. I had left Theresa with her few blanket tied possessions, and was grasping my own burlap bags, barely moving through the crowd, when a member of the crew took my arm. "Second class will be leaving next, Miss," he said guiding me along.

"But I need to speak to someone in third class."

"Third class has to go through inspection, Miss. It will be hours before they go ashore."

My heart sank. I was losing my only friend in America. When I caught up with Theresa, she was frantic. "Tom's not getting off with us. He didn't know where he'd be staying, and I don't know where I'm heading."

When the tender reached the dock, Theresa was sniffling. As we walked along the wooden planks the steaming air smelled so much of tar and fish, I struggled to catch my breath. It seemed half of Ireland really was in Boston, as laughing and crying relatives and friends greeted each other.

Slowly, the crowd thinned, and I saw her. She was nothing like I had pictured in my shipboard reveries, yet I knew without a doubt, I was looking at my aunt, Delia Reardon.

CHAPTER 13

Like Gran, my Aunt Delia was tall and slim, with a thin nose that kept her a shade away from being beautiful. Her black hair was swept up, and wings of gray at the sides seemed to continue on and blend into the feathers of her hat. In a dove gray dress she looked as stylish as the ladies from first class. Despite the stifling heat, much worse than I'd ever felt in Ireland, she wore gloves.

For a full half-minute I stared, unable to move forward. When Theresa clutched my arm I whispered, "That's my aunt Delia. Over by the carriage, waiting for us."

But Theresa wasn't looking toward my aunt. Pulling away, she said through tears, "We can't be leaving before Tom gets off the ship. We can't." As I practically dragged her along, she looked back at the *Halcyon*, as if she was being torn away from home.

My aunt made no attempt to approach us, and by the time we were in front of her, I was still at a loss for words. She leaned forward and kissed me lightly on the forehead. "Welcome to America, Mary." In exactly the same tone, she welcomed Theresa, adding, "I hope you will find your position to your liking."

When she told the driver to take our bags, Theresa burst into tears. "There's...there's those me and Mary have to say goodbye to, Ma'am. We can't be leaving till third class comes off."

My aunt drew herself taller, a habit of Gran's when she was displeased. "Ship board friendships are soon forgotten, and getting through third class takes forever. It's one of the reasons I sent fares for second cabin."

As we climbed into the carriage, I whispered to Theresa, "Mrs. Moriarity will give Tom her son's address. She'll tell Tom to write to her there as soon as he knows where he's staying." I added with more confidence than I felt, "And we can find where Petey Moriarity lives. Mrs. Moriarity said his name is known all over Boston."

Delia Reardon took the seat across from us. Theresa sat with her hands clenched in her lap. I had to look away, thinking how Aggie would have welcomed us with hugs and smiles and a flurry of questions. "Had we enjoyed the trip? Had we been comfortable?"

The silence in the carriage was awkward, so I stared at the market stalls and pushcarts lining the streets. Soon we passed buildings which rose like walls on either side, some so high that when I craned my neck I still couldn't see the sky. Horses pulled carriages carrying dozens of people along metal rails. I felt I had arrived in another world.

As we passed a huge building with a golden dome, my aunt said crisply, like a schoolteacher instructing a classroom of pupils," The gold dome is the State Capitol. Across the street is The Boston Common."

"Thank you," I replied. "I was wondering what it was."

I could not tell from my aunt's expression whether she was pleased or disappointed with either of us. As the wheels clacked over the stones and the horses' hooves clip-clopped rhythmically, I told myself silently, "Delia is fair…Delia is intelligent." And then like an echo I'd hear, "Heart of stone. Heart of stone."

The carriage entered a narrow street. We went slowly uphill, tilted backward against the horsehide seats, past rows of red brick houses. After another turn the carriage stopped in front of an end house with a carefully trimmed hedge behind an iron fence. A path of bricks led to a black door with a gleaming brass knocker.

But we didn't enter the front door. Instead, with the driver carrying our bags, we opened a small gate, followed a path along the side of the house, walked down a few steps, and opened a door. A rush of heat greeted us. At the end of a narrow passage, we came to a kitchen with a huge stove blasting.

My aunt told the driver, "Take the girls' baggage upstairs, but hurry down. And don't let the stable tell you we were gone more than two hours." She motioned to a square table. "Sit here. Marie will bring you something to drink." With that she left the kitchen.

A minute later an aproned woman with a pretty face appeared carrying a tray holding two glasses of lemonade. Chips of ice clinked against the sides, even though it was summer. "It's no day for an oven to be blasting, but I've a pound cake almost ready. It should be a treat after what you've been getting on board the ship." A bell rang and she turned to a half-closed door, calling, "Cissy, pour a glass of lemonade from the pitcher in the ice box, and take it upstairs."

A frail and homely younger woman appeared and glanced at us timidly. In an almost childlike voice, she wailed, "Mama, you said I wouldn't have to go up to her anymore." I was surprised that she had called the woman who was obviously the cook "Mama". They looked nothing alike. There did not seem to be enough difference in their ages.

"It's just this once Cissy. Go on now, she won't bite you."

When Cissy reappeared carrying a tray her mother, cautioned, "Make sure to ask if there's anything else she wants. Don't give Lady High-and-Mighty a chance to criticize."

I looked at Theresa for a sign of what she made of the odd exchange, but she was staring out a window on a level with the ground outside. Lost in thoughts of Tom, no doubt. I drained my glass, hoping my aunt wasn't Lady High-and-Mighty, and that someone else in the house had put Cissy in a panic.

Marie asked if the crossing had been rough, and was the food terrible, as it had been when she'd crossed thirty years before during the worst of the famine. When I said the meals hadn't been too bad, she laughed. "Well, you'll soon be having the finest meals in Boston. My late husband was head chef in the finest hotel in Quebec. Marcel, rest his soul, was trained in Paris, France. But I haven't forgotten the way with simple meals."

She was so easy to talk to I began to relax. By the time she removed a golden pound cake from the oven. I had almost forgotten the name, Lady High-and-Mighty. Then my aunt returned wearing a severe black dress. Without her hat, her hair was a mass of almost coal black waves except for the gray sides. She glanced at the cake cooling on a rack. "Dust the top with confectioner's sugar, Marie," she said, and motioned to us to follow her.

I was curious to see more of Delia's house. But instead of looking around the first floor, we went up a back stairway. At each landing the temperature rose. After the fourth flight, we walked down a windowless hall. She opened the door to a small room. An iron bedstead, single chair, and a small bureau, holding a basin and chipped pitcher took up most of the space. Theresa's bundle was on the floor beneath an open window. A white cotton dress with narrow pale green stripes lay across the bed next to an apron and a starched cap. "Change into these, Theresa," Delia said. "And make sure your hair is well brushed and tucked in neatly." She turned to me. "Your room is across the hall."

Why would I be sleeping so high up in such a big house, I wondered. But when Delia opened the door to my room, I saw an identical bedstead and washstand, an identical dress and apron and cap.

I was dumbstruck. My aunt had sent for me to be a maid in her fine house.

CHAPTER 14

Delia walked in ahead of me and pulled down a green window shade. "This will cut off the afternoon sun. We're having a heat wave, but it should cool off later in the evening." She crossed the room and opened another door. "Our rooms connect. You can shut your door but you might like to sit in my room to read where there's good lamplight."

I followed her into a bedroom where a stack of books and an ornate lamp stood on a marble-topped table. On either side of the table there were two comfortable chairs. Bewildered, I asked, "Why do you choose to sleep way up here? There's so much room in this house."

"I've grown used to the stairs," she replied. She must have noticed the confusion on my face. "Mary, do you think I own this house?"

When I nodded, she swept her hand across her hair and shook her head. "I've said nothing to mislead you. Whatever gave you such an idea?"

I stumbled over my words. "The cabin class tickets. You coming in a carriage and all, and the way you were dressed."

"There was nothing in my letters."

My mind spinning, I stammered, "You sent money for second cabin." I paused for a breath. "Gran thought you were doing well, though she didn't actually say...." I stopped, not wanting to reveal that her mother had never talked about her. I waited for Delia to ask how Gran was. What she'd thought of my going off.

But my aunt's next words were, "I promised that you'd get a fine education, Mary, and you will." She lifted several of the books from the marble topped table. "I've taken these from the library for you. Tonight you can choose whichever you want to read first. Now, maybe you'd like to go into your room and rest awhile."

I was being dismissed.

Before she closed the door between our rooms she spoke less abruptly. "You don't need to change into your uniform until morning. Cissy will tap on your door and let you know when we'll be eating tonight."

I removed my dress and lay on the bed in my shift. . The drawn shade hadn't helped. The room was still hot. I had never thought that I wouldn't appreciate a sunny day, but a rainstorm would have been welcome. Across the hall, I heard Theresa opening and shutting drawers. Her room could be no hotter than mine. I might as well go in and talk with her.

She had changed into her uniform and was staring out at the back of a brick building as tall as the one we were in. A small alley ran between the two buildings.

"The uniform looks nice on you," I said.

"The heat in this country is wicked," she answered, sniffling.

"My aunt says it's a heat wave and will soon be over."

Theresa turned from the window and wiped her eyes. "It's going to be strange, having a place for my own things, all so neat and clean." She walked over to the bed and touched the cotton spread. Then she burst into a torrent of tears.. "Maybe it was like your aunt said, Mary. Just a shipboard friendship, but I'll never forget Tom as long as I live."

"Tom won't be forgetting you, either." I sat on the bed beside her, glad to be thinking about something other than my aunt. "Remember, how he looked at you when he was singing Rose of Tralee? Didn't he take you up to first class, have you sitting with Mr. And Mrs. O'Connor as if you two were a couple already? He'll be trying to find you, as hard as we'll be looking for him."

"Boston is a vast city, Mary. Where would we begin?"

"We'll be going to church Sunday. Have the priest put your name down as a new member of the parish. Tom may be giving his name to another church. Then we'll ask if anybody has heard of Peter Moriarity. It's not a common name."

Theresa clenched her hands, taking in every word, as if determination alone would help us find Tom. I left her washing her face at the flowered basin, which she'd filled with water from a matching pitcher on her marble stand.

As I washed my own face, I noticed that the washcloth was new. That like Theresa, I had an inkwell and pen, stamps, and even writing paper and envelopes. When Cissy tapped at the door and timidly announced it was time for dinner, I realized I was hungry.

We ate a salad of cold flaked haddock, layered between peas and cucumber, a combination I would never have thought of. It was surprisingly good. Cissy beamed as if she'd made the meal herself. Homely as she was, when her face lit up, she was pleasing to look at, and she didn't seem in the least afraid of my aunt. But when a bell rang in the kitchen, she turned pale, and I realized that from somewhere above Lady High-and-Mighty was calling. Her mother nodded and Cissy rose from her half finished meal and left the room.

When I finished eating, Deliia showed me the downstairs. The rooms were small in comparison to Ashmont. Every surface was crowded with objects, and heavy draperies kept out much of the fading daylight.

"It's seldom used, but this room must be dusted everyday. The lamps lighted for two hours each night" Delia said as she struck a match and lit an oil lamp. "Every morning these wicks are to be trimmed and the chimneys taken off and washed."

Over the mantle a full-length portrait of a young girl was the only object in the room that struck me as beautiful. As if she'd read my mind Delia said, "That's Mrs. Wooley as a girl. In the morning you'll meet her. She fancies herself bedridden and it would be better never to contradict her."

She led us to the next room where the painting of a round, jolly looking man, hung opposite a portrait of a beautiful woman with rings and necklace and a somewhat haughty air. "Mrs. Wooley, again," my aunt explained. In a gentler voice she added, "Mr. Wooley died three years ago."

Mrs. Wooley had to be the Lady High-and-Mighty, who'd had Cissy almost in tears. I met the portrait's haughty gaze with a firm one of my own, and decided then and there that I would not be intimidated.

∞

That night we sat in Aunt Delia's room, in small but comfortable chairs. The oil lamp on the table between us cast a soft glow over a pot of tea, a plate of biscuits (which my aunt called cookies) and several books.

We sipped tea and ate the crisp lemon cookies, as my aunt talked about impersonal things. The size of Boston, and its early history. The Public Garden, which now had boats shaped like swans that children delighted in. A public library with two hundred and fifty thousand books. She used many words where I had to guess at the meaning.

When I yawned and rubbed my eyes, Delia suggested, "You've had a long day, Mary. You should go to bed." She put a book into my hand. *Little Women* is popular with young girls. Perhaps tomorrow night you can start it."

I didn't light either the small lamp or the candle in my own room, but undressed in what I thought was the light from a full moon. But when I drew aside the cotton curtain, hoping for a breeze, through the leaves of a maple tree, I saw a glowing street lamp. What a rich city Boston must be, I thought, lighting the streets when most people were asleep.

Directly opposite, on a level with my own room, an older woman moved slowly in the dim light then pulled down the shade on her window. I wondered if she had come over from Ireland after the famine. And had she hated working in someone else's house, sleeping in a hot room in summer, probably a cold room in winter, then dream each night of the green fields back home?

I stood for a long time, not knowing which I felt more. Disappointment, anger or shame? Gran had sent me off to be a student in a fine Boston school. How would I explain that I was a maid in a house where Delia was the housekeeper?

I climbed into bed and pulled a sheet over me. Minutes later I tossed it off: the room was too hot for even a thin sheet. In the unaccustomed silence, I lay awake, missing the sound of the waves I'd fallen to sleep to all my life. And wondering about my aunt.

She had talked all evening, and told me many interesting things, but hadn't asked one question about Gran, or anyone else in Ballydare

Delia Reardon was as much a mystery as ever.

CHAPTER 15

Mrs. Trottier set poached eggs, crisp bacon, toast and tea in front of us. "A real Irish breakfast, will taste good after what they fed you on the ship."

Theresa and I thanked her, and as I finished the last bite of toast my aunt came into the kitchen and asked me to stand up. She handed me a rolled up a tea towel "The uniform is the right length, but tuck this down the front. Tonight, I'll take it in for a better fit."

As I blushed furiously, Mrs. Trottier said to my aunt, "The old lady won't notice she hasn't filled out, as long as her tea comes in hot."

"She looks too young and it's only for the first meeting. After that Theresa will be the one going upstairs," Delia explained.

With my face still flaming, I turned my back, stuffed the rolled linen down the front of my uniform, and then smoothed the apron bib.

Delia handed Theresa a tray and we followed her up the servants' staircase. Theresa's uniform, handed down from a girl who'd just left, was a perfect fit. Mine, though stiff with starch, hung on me shapelessly and with every step the towel shifted. We left the backstairs and crossed a wide hall to a bedroom in the front of the house.

"I've brought the new girls up, Ma'am. Mary and Theresa," my aunt called in softly.

A figure stirred in the middle of the bed. A thin old woman sat up and glared. "Draw back the curtains, Delia. I can hardly see them," she commanded in a clear flute like tone. As my aunt pulled aside the soft cream-colored curtains the woman squinted toward us. "Can you read and write?" Both Theresa and I nodded. "Speak up. I can barely hear you?"

I felt the towel slip to one side. Remembering my determination not to be intimidated, I squared my shoulders and answered promptly, "I read well, and my penmanship is quite clear."

She turned toward Theresa. "And you?"

Theresa, the tray shaking in her hand, answered in little more than a whisper. "My handwriting is very neat."

Mrs. Wooley turned then toward Delia who was straightening magazines on the bedside table. "I'll not have another illiterate like Bridget, who couldn't even hand me the right magazine."

Delia answered calmly. "It will be Theresa coming now. And if that is all, I'll take the girls around and show them their duties."

Mrs. Wooley called after us, "Count the silver, Delia. I wouldn't be surprised if Bridget took a few pieces."

As soon as we were on the staircase my aunt whispered, " There's been no Bridget for two years, and the last girl, Anna, wouldn't take so much as a teaspoon. It's a waste of time, but we'll count the silver later in the day."

I was set to sweeping a feather duster across an intricately carved piece of furniture my aunt called a hall tree. In its mirror, I saw the lopsided tea towel and pulled it out. I stared at myself in the ill-fitting uniform, recalling the time I'd stood in front of my grandmother's smaller mirror, a white towel draped around my forehead and a black shawl over my head to see how I'd look as a missionary sister. I'd had the good sense to know being pleased at my appearance was not the sign of a religious vocation. Another time, wrapped in my grandmothers black shawl, I'd pretended to warn everyone, "Plant turnips and cabbages along with the potatoes," thus saving the whole of Ballydare from famine.

But never had I pictured myself in a maid's uniform with a silly cap and a feather duster.

At the sound of footsteps, I swept the feathers quickly over the hall tree. "You're barely moving the dust," my aunt said, taking the duster from my hand.

"There's no dust to see," I protested.

"That's because it's done every day."

It hardly seemed logical, but I didn't argue as she finished dusting the stand herself. Later, Delia handed us flannel bags, saying, "Mary, you count the oyster forks, while Theresa counts the demitasse spoons."

"Why would anyone need a special fork to eat an oyster?" I asked as I laid the oddly shaped forks in a row.

"It's the way things are done in a household like this. You'll want to know such things when you've a household of your own." When Theresa commented on how beautiful the demi taste spoons were, my aunt agreed, but corrected her. "It's demitasse, Theresa, not demi taste." Theresa's lips moved as she repeated the word. I could see that my aunt was pleased with her interest. Next Delia showed us cups and saucers so thin I could almost see through them, warning, "Be careful. These are Havilland china."

Theresa exclaimed at how lovely they were. I said nothing. Was I to be learning about oyster forks, and china that broke easily, instead of going to school?

When Cissy called in, "The bell's ringing," Delia offered to go up with Theresa on her first day. I followed Cissy into the kitchen. At a loud clap of thunder, followed by a flash, she shook so hard, her mother sent her to the pantry so she wouldn't see the lightening.

"Cissy's afraid of her shadow," Mrs. Trottier explained. "After she came down with a fever on the ship, she was never the same." She ran her hands over her arms. "It still sends a shiver when I remember that trip, us all crammed together like a school of mackerel. And conditions no better when we were held on Grosse Isle. The Canadians were afraid we'd spread the fever to the mainland."

With a pot of tea, a plate of biscuits, and rain falling in sheets outside, it was almost like being back with Gran listening to a neighbor as Marie Trottier told how she and her brother Joe were the only ones out of their whole family to survive the famine. The landlord paid their passage to Canada, but it was not simply generosity on his part. It was becoming more profitable to clear the land and raise cattle. In the crossing, Joe died of small pox and Marie was left with no family. The Ryans, Cissy's parents, said she could stay in Canada with them. Then the Ryans took sick. Mr. Ryan died first, then Mrs. Ryan.

Marie glanced at the closed pantry door. The thunder was now a distant rumble. "I can still hear Mary Ryan crying, 'What will become of the poor babe?' I promised her I'd care for Cissy as if she was my own. I was but fifteen. But I've done it. And thanks to your aunt, God bless her, she'll be cared for after I'm gone."

She reached across the table and placed her hand on mine. "Your aunt can have a sharp tongue at times, Mary. How she holds it with the old lady I don't know. But ever since she's known you were coming, she's thought of nothing else. She had the rooms on the top floor painted. Moved her sewing things, so you'd be in the room next to her. I know she has great plans for you." At the sound of footsteps on the servant's stairs, she patted my hand lightly, "We'll talk later."

Delia had changed from the plain black dress into an outfit as elegant as the one she'd worn the day before. She handed me a sheet of paper and a stamped envelope addressed to Ballydare. The return address was on the back.

"There's pen and ink on the shelf. Write a quick note saying you've arrived safely. I'll mail it on my way to town. When you've finished, gather the clothes you wore on the boat for Mrs. Rafferty to wash tomorrow. You'll need clean clothes for Mass Sunday."

With Delia standing at the end of the table impatiently tapping her fingers, I wrote my first letter to my Grandmother.

>*Dear Gran,*
>
>   *Yesterday we arrived safely in Boston. Aunt Delia met us at the dock and I recognized her right away. She looks a lot like you. She did not want you to worry, so she is having me send a quick note that she will mail right away. We will be going to Mass together on Sunday. Tell Aunt Aggie I love the striped dress best I will write you a real letter soon.*
>
>   *Your loving granddaughter,*
>   *Mary*

I had expected my first letter to be filled with news about the trip, and Delia, and Boston. But at least in my quick note I'd told Gran how Delia looked, and that we'd be going to church together. She'd be reassured knowing Delia hadn't lost the faith.

I couldn't possibly have written that I was living with a horrible old woman who scared the servants. That I'd spent the day counting silver because she was sure some had been stolen. And that I'd stuffed a towel inside my uniform so I'd look old enough to work as a maid.

As soon as Delia left, Theresa came in, her eyes shining. "I've had a sign, Mary. Right after I asked for one, I found this brand new penny lying heads up on the floor. She sing- songed, *See a penny, pick it up and you're sure to have good luck. See a penny let it lie and good luck will pass you by."*

Gran always said "See a pin and pick it up" because she wouldn't have wasted a common straight pin. However, I wasn't going to dash Theresa's hopes.

"I'll light a candle with this penny, Sunday," she said then. "I'll ask to be seeing Tom within the week."

"Or ask for another sign," I suggested. "I haven't thought of any new ways to find him."

"There _has_ to be a way, Mary. Tom is the only one I could ever love." She broke down in tears. "Now that I've met Tom Kerrigan there'll never be another for me."

Cissy rushed from the pantry and put her arms around Theresa. "I'll light a candle myself for you and your young man. Mama will, too. Won't you Mama?"

"Of course, Cissy. When the three of us go to nine o'clock Mass." She turned to me. "There's always someone left home, and your aunt usually goes to eleven."

I left Theresa stringing beans and talking about Tom Kerrigan, and went up for the clothes that needed washing.

First I would have to rip open a few stitches in the waist of my dress and remove the money I had hidden there. Seeing Delia's door open, I went in for the small scissors she kept on the marble-topped table. A pin cushion with a needle and thread long enough to close the seam lay next to the scissors. When I lifted the cushion I glimpsed a sheet of paper with a list of Irish names, followed by numbers. But it was the heading that caught my eye. *Emerald*

Row. I had heard the name before.

As I sat cross-legged in the center of my bed carefully cutting stitches, I remembered Mrs. Moriarity's words to Ned Kelley. "There's hardly a day goes by someone from Ann Street or Emerald Row isn't hauled before the judge."

Ann Street and Emerald Row seemed a world apart from the quiet street beyond my window. It would take awhile before the passage money back to Ireland and Emerald Row came together again in my mind.

CHAPTER 16

As I put my dresses into Mrs. Rafferty's rough red hands the next morning, I thought that even cutting turf or digging potatoes would be better than scrubbing clothes every day. Theresa handed the laundress her green dress asking, "Are you sure it won't shrink?"

"I've not ruined a stitch of clothing in twenty years." Mrs. Rafferty said huffily, as if she'd been insulted. She held the dress out at arms length. "I'll soak it in cold salt water so the colors don't run. Tomorrow when I iron it, the dress will look as good as new." She resumed rubbing lye soap over the sheets on the washboard, and I left the steaming laundry room for a breath of air.

As I swept the duster across the hall tree in the front hall I kept the front door open, and glanced longingly at the trees that lined the street. If only I could walk away for a few hours. See and hear what lay beyond Sabine Street.

A few stray duster feathers landed on a small rug. I was about to pick it up and give it a few shakes out the door, when half a dozen pigeons fluttered down from the eaves to peck among the bushes. I'd not had a close look at these city birds before, so I went to the kitchen and found a dry roll left over from breakfast.

From the front steps I threw crumbs tempting the cautious birds to come closer. A light breeze held a faint trace of the sea, and I closed my eyes, pretending the pigeons were the geese I'd fed every morning.

I was startled by my aunt's sharp voice as she came up the

walk. "Good heavens, Mary. Get inside. This isn't a cottage in Ballydare. Next thing you're likely to be shaking the rug out the door." She shook her head, as if she'd witnessed a crime.

I followed her inside, hurt and angry. She must have fed geese a thousand times, shaken scatter rugs out the door in Ireland and never thought a thing of it. Had America changed her so much she thought work had to be hidden?

Later, as I dusted the parlor windowsills, I looked across the street at the glistening window panes, gleaming door knockers, and swept walks. All the work of maids and chore men. Was Boston that different from Ireland?

Aggie once said when her father was seen wheeling clippings past a window at Ashmont, he'd been scolded and sent half a mile out of his way to dispose of them. Her mother had filled Ashmont's vases in the early hours to make it appear fresh flowers arrived miraculously without a lick of work.

I turned from the window, wondering if the only time I'd see what lay beyond Sabine Street was going to Mass on Sunday mornings.

∞

I was ready by ten thirty. When Theresa and Marie Trottier and Cissy returned from the earlier Mass, Theresa dropped onto a kitchen chair and groaned. "I've never walked so far in shoes before. Wait 'til you see St. Joseph's, Mary. It doesn't look catholic till you get inside, because it used to be a protestant church. But after the bishop bought it, he blessed it and made it all right to go in. You'll see our candles on the top row, right in the center."

Cissy rested her hand on Theresa's shoulder. "You've done all you can, Miss. I'm sure your Tom will be finding his way here soon."

When Theresa left I told Cissy how nice she looked. Her soft rose dress added color to her pale skin, the ruffles and tucks flattered her thin frame.

"Miss Reardon made this dress for me for my thirty-second birthday. She says rose is my color." Her mother's hint of a smile suggested this was another example of my aunt's good qualities.

Delia came into the kitchen in the dress she worn at the dock and a hat that was even more elegant. "Mary, we'd better hurry or we'll be late," she said looking me over as if to see if I was properly dressed for Mass.

As we walked side by side up the steep hill, she nodded to a few girls who passed at a quicker pace. After we crested the hill, the bricks became uneven. Doorways needed painting. Scraps of paper clung to rusty iron fencing. By the bottom of the hill, the trimmed bushes were gone, and piles of ashes lay scattered in patches of sparse grass.

I was glad I'd been forewarned. St. Joseph's was a different sort of building for a church, low, square, and plain. However, inside I felt right at home with the statues of Mary and Joseph on either side of the altar, and the blend of incense and candles. I checked the top row and saw the three vigil lights burning for Tom.

Although I tried to pay attention I caught myself noticing that only the oldest women wore shawls. The young women without children were the best dressed. Probably servants, living in, with few expenses. I recognized no one from the ship.

After Mass, Delia nodded to a few people, but spoke only with a ruddy-faced priest, who sounded as if he'd arrived on the *Halcyon*.

"So, Miss Reardon, this is your niece." he said with a smile. "How do you like our fair city, Mary?"

I was flustered, and my aunt filled in quickly. "She's not seen much of it yet, Father Flynn, but sometime soon we'll make a day of it, won't we, Mary?"

"I'd like that," I agreed, hoping she meant it.

Halfway up the north side of the hill, Delia asked, "Have you read much of Little Women?"

"I finished it."

"Really! And did you like it?"

"I thought it was very good, except when they talked about being poor, even though they had a cook. That seemed strange." I hesitated. After all, my aunt had chosen the book for me. She must have thought it was good.

Delia looked at me with great interest. "Go on."

"Well..." I paused to gather my thoughts. "I think Louisa

May Alcott said Jo did things in a gentlemanly manner too many times. She didn't need to say it more than once or twice."

My aunt laughed. Whatever my shortcomings with the feather duster, I had pleased her. "We'll get you a library card," she said. "You're more ready than I realized."

As we picked our way with cautious steps down the steepest part of the hill, I wondered. *What did Delia think I was ready for?*

CHAPTER 17

Two mornings later, as I swished a cloth across the rose- painted oil lamp chimney in the parlor, my aunt came down the front staircase carrying a large round box. She had changed from her plain black dress into a blue dress as elegant as the one she'd worn when she met us at the wharf. When she stopped in front of the hall mirror to arrange her hat, I walked to the doorway, hoping she'd tell me to come with her. Maybe, as we walked, I could finally lead the conversation around to Ballydare and Gran.

However, when the feathered hat was positioned to her satisfaction, she smiled, picked up the round box and said goodbye. Disappointed, I watched her walk briskly down the brick path, and resumed my boring parlor chores. When I saw a man striding up the path, I returned to the front hall, smoothed my apron, and opened the door.

A heavy-set man with a bulldog face demanded, in a voice with more than a trace of Ireland, "I want to speak with Miss Reardon."

"Miss Reardon has gone out," I answered. I suspected I was supposed to add, "Sir", but I couldn't bring myself to say it to a man who sounded so rude.

"When will she back?"

"That I don't know. But I can tell her you came to call." He looked at me with a scowl, then down at a thick envelope he was holding. "If there's something you wish to leave for her, I can see that she gets it,." I said as pleasantly as I could. When he still hesitated, I added. "I'm her niece. I'll put it on her table where she will be sure to see it."

"And you be sure that you do." He thrust the envelope into my hand, turned and left.

Immediately, I went up to my aunt's room, placed the envelope next to a ring of keys in the center of the marble topped table, and went downstairs to finish the what seemed like endless, useless dusting.

Theresa was unusually quiet at the noon meal. When Marie asked her, "What do you plan to do on your afternoon off, now that you've a few dollars in your pocket?" she shrugged listlessly. "You could let Cissy show you the shops, unless you want to sit in your room all day."

Theresa went pale. "Oh, no. I wouldn't want to do that."

After she left with Cissy, Marie rested her arms on the back of a chair. "A trip to town
will do both girls a world of good. Theresa does like to talk and is likely a bit homesick, and Cissy has never had a friend before." The cook sighed. " I'd hate to see Theresa leave because the old lady can have a very sharp tongue. She's driven off a dozen girls in the three years Mr. Wooley's been gone. The old gentleman had a way of smoothing things over."

She rose, went to the pantry, and returned with an apron full of peas to be shelled. As the tiny peas rattled our pans, Marie explained the way the household had once been run.

"Now, it's just seven people, including Mrs. Rafferty who comes in two days a week to do the laundry, and a part time chore man. That should be enough help for one woman in a town house. But she wants it run as if there's still twice that in help."

"She must be rich to be paying so many people," I said.

"There are far richer in Boston," the cook replied. "But none more demanding,."

From the rest of the conversation, I figured the Wooleys to be an odd family. Mrs. Trottier referred to Mrs. Wooley's middle aged son, George, as "that poor boy," and pitied his wife, Dorothy, who had always been polite and considerate to servants when they'd lived on Sabine Street. But there had always been friction: The older Mrs. Wooley disapproved of her son's wife, because

Dorothy attended lectures by Lucy Stone, and read The Woman's Journal which printed articles about allowing women to vote, and the dangerous effects of tight corsets. Mrs.Wooley never visited them once they moved to Chestnut Hill.

"Even Mrs. Rafferty has her doubts about a magazine that tells women not to wear corsets." Mrs. Trottier said as we pared potatoes together, "She says she'd never go to church without a corset because she wouldn't feel decent."

By the time I started my afternoon duty of washing lamp chimneys that didn't need cleaning, I knew there was no place like a kitchen to learn what went on in families, whether in Boston or Ballydare.

I was back in the kitchen for a glass of lemonade, when a wagon rattled to a stop in the alley. Marie opened the door to a wiry young man carrying a block of ice between huge tongs. As she made a stabbing gesture with her hand, he chopped some slivers from the block. Marie gave him a coin from a jar on a shelf. "For you. Tip"

"Tip," he repeated. "For chop de ice. I thank you, Mrs." he replied.

As the wagon rolled off, she said, "Gestures can do wonders. I'd not a word of French stranded as I was on Grosse Isle. Then a young doctor pointed to me and the baby, and handed me an address where I might find room and board in exchange for helping in the house. He'd stayed at Madame Trottier's when he was a medical student in Montreal."

"*Madame Trottier!* That's your name now. Did you marry her son?" I broke in, pleased to hear a happy turn to Marie's story.

"No, Marcel was her brother. The French refer to unmarried women after a certain age as Madame. He came for dinner on Sundays." Her eyes took on a far away look as she scraped. "Soon Marcel was staying later and later. One Sunday he carried a dusty pram up from the basement. He washed it and we went out that afternoon. He pushed the pram. I walked beside him, knowing I'd be marrying him, though he never did ask me in so many words."

The bell jangled on the board overhead. She stood up. "I'll slip ice into some raspberry shrub. Ask if there's anything else she wants."

I'd not seen Mrs. Wooley since the first morning. I told myself that if she snapped at me, I wouldn't let it bother me. Still, I winced when the door squeaked as I opened it.

The old lady was sitting in the bed surrounded by pillows. Without raising her eyes from the page, she said, "Godey's Ladies Book has fallen to the floor."

I set the glass on the table. As I handed her the magazine, she nodded, and if the grunt she gave was a thank you, I wasn't sure.

"Is there anything else you'll be wanting?" I asked.

She shook her head, and I left. Mrs.Wooley hadn't once looked at me. A harsh word wouldn't have felt any ruder.

When Theresa and Cissy returned, Theresa showed off a new hat with a cluster of flowers, a hat pin with a mother-of-pearl top, and a pair of white cotton gloves.

"You must have spent every cent," I said..

"I really needed these things, Mary. I saved something for the collection plate and a candle next Sunday. I'll send a bit of my wages home next week."

Delia frowned at Theresa over her spectacle rims. But when I passed my aunt in the hall she smiled. "If tomorrow is a nice day, put on a dress in the morning and we'll go into town. We'll stop by the library and you can get a library card."

That night as I laid my blue dress over the back of the one chair so I'd be ready in the morning, there was a timid knock, and Theresa opened the door "Can I sit with you a while, Mary?"

I removed my dress from the chair, but she sat on the bed. As she described the expensive stores, the way people were dressed, I was afraid she'd rattle on endlessly, the way she did about Tom. But when she started fidgeting with the edge of the cotton spread and seemed to be thinking of new things to say, I asked, "What's wrong, Theresa?"

She glanced toward the closed door to my aunt's room. "Didn't this room used to be your aunt's sewing room?"

"It was," I answered, waiting.

"So it was my room the girls slept in?" She bit her lip. "When did Mr. Wooly die?"

"Three years ago."

"And since then no girl has stayed on more than a few months?"

Still smarting from the way the old lady hadn't glanced in my direction that afternoon, I answered, "Mrs. Wooley is rude and inconsiderate and has driven them away."

Theresa looked down at her clasped hands. "It's not her that's driven the live-in girls away, Mary." Her lips were quivering. "It's the haunt in the attic, right over my bed. I heard it last night."

"Don't be silly, Theresa. You probably heard a squirrel running across the roof."

"It was no squirrel. It was footsteps, as if someone was looking for something. Are you sure you didn't hear anything?"

"The only thing I've heard at night is a carriage going by. Once I may have heard a squirrel."

"It was *not* a squirrel. These were footsteps going up the attic stairs, creaking across the floorboards right over my head Quiet and ghostly like." She was shivering. "Maybe the old gentleman is a lost soul come back and can't rest in peace."

"It's either a squirrel or the house creaking." I insisted. "And don't talk about haunts and ghostly footsteps, Theresa. They'll think you're nothing more than a silly girl. Someday, I'll go up with you and we'll look around."

I left her still trembling and returned with *"Little Women"* hoping a book would take her mind off ghosts. "You should read this," I said as I placed the book on her bureau. She barely looked up and I added, "Tomorrow we'll know there's nothing wrong."

But even as I said it, I felt a tingle on the back of my neck and the hair rise on my arms.

CHAPTER 18

I tried the attic door the next morning and found it locked. My aunt kept a ring of keys on her bedside table, but I couldn't ask her for the key. She'd think Theresa's talk of footsteps and ghostly sounds were nonsense.

When we were alone in the first floor hallway, Theresa didn't mention the attic, and I hoped that maybe she had come to her senses. As my aunt passed us, dressed for town, she said, "I'll be ready to leave for town in twenty minutes, Mary."

Since I was wearing what I thought of as my "real clothes," I decided to walk up Sabine Street in the direction I hadn't taken on Sunday morning. Careful not to stare like some gawking country girl, I walked quickly as if I had a destination, and then turned back. My heart sank when I saw a well-dressed man and a girl about my own age helping a little boy out of a carriage. Would our trip into town be canceled?

I cut into the passage that ran to the back of the house. As I entered the kitchen, Marie Trottier put a finger to her lips. Voices in the hall were subdued, then my aunt came into the room with the girl and little boy I had seen in front of the house, and asked, "Marie, will you make those lemon cookies the children like while their grandmother finishes dressing?"

Cissy took the little boy into the back yard. Her mother reached for a mixing bowl, commenting, "My, how you both have grown."

"Oh don't remind me," the girl answered. "I'm afraid I'll be as tall as my Aunt Esther." She turned to me with a smile. "I'm Ellen Wooley, Mrs. Wooley's granddaughter."

"I'm Mary Cleary, Delia Reardon's niece," I replied, thinking how unlike her grandmother the girl was.

"Have you had a chance to see much of Boston?"

All I could think to answer was, "Not yet." I hesitated, wondering if the plain but intelligent looking girl was simply being polite. But she was looking at me with such interest, I added, "My aunt gave me a book about a family that lived near Boston. *Little Women.*"

"I read *Little Women* right before I met Louisa May Alcott."

"You actually met her!"

She laughed. "I knew that would impress you. It does everyone."

"Was she anything like Jo? I mean, the way Jo would be when she grew up."

Ellen Wooley's high forehead creased. "She's nothing like Jo. In fact, when she came here she seemed quite difficult and cross."

"Louisa May Alcott was *here? In this house?*"

"She came to a tea for the New England Woman's Club. I was surprised such an unpleasant woman could write such a nice book. After she left, Mrs. Cotton said she suspected Miss Alcott was laced."

I'd heard of lacing a punch with whiskey. My regard for Louisa May Alcott was sinking rapidly until Ellen added, "Being laced up in a corset is disapproved of by the club committee on dress reform."

As the fragrance of drop cookies filled the air, we were discussing whether Miss Alcott was less like sweet, suffering Beth and more like self-centered Amy when Delia called from the doorway, "Your Grandmother is ready to see you and Andrew in the parlor."

A shadow crossed Ellen's face when Cissy brought the little boy inside. "I hope Andrew's hands are clean enough to go into the parlor."

"You go on ahead," Mrs. Trottier said. "I'll make him presentable." She lifted the little boy onto a chair at the sink, and washed his hands and face. "Stay with him," she said as she handed him to me. "If he breaks anything, we'll never hear the end of it."

Mrs. Wooley was sitting beneath the portrait of herself as a young girl. There was only a sad resemblance. Her son sat opposite, Ellen between them by the front window. As they discussed the hot weather in chilly tones, I wondered what had gone wrong.

Mrs. Wooley scowled at me. "What are you doing out of your uniform?"

"It's my day off, Ma'am," I replied, and caught Ellen's look of surprise at learning I was a maid in her grandmother's house. Suddenly Andrew pulled away from me. Before I could stop him he grabbed a small porcelain bulldog, crying with delight, "Buster! My dog." He ran toward his father and tripped. The dog shattered at his feet.

"I see Dorothy hasn't taught Andrew not to touch things in other peoples' houses." There was a twitch around the old woman's mouth, as if she were glad for the chance to criticize. "But then she wouldn't have time, running off to meetings about women and their rights."

Her son rose and picked up his crying son. "I thought for once we could spend a pleasant hour together, Mother. But in the short time we've been here, you've told Ellen the color of her dress doesn't suit her, implying her mother is lacking in taste. You've asked if I'm pale because I find traveling into the city a strain."

"Well, you know it was a foolish move."

"It was a *necessary* move, Mother. You and my wife can't live under the same roof. You've even turned a child's accident into Dorothy's fault."

I backed out of the parlor. Ellen followed her father and little brother, dabbing at her eyes.

Delia was already in the hall. "Whatever happened in there, you mustn't blame yourselves. Your mother is having a hard time since your father died. This is a big house and a lot to manage."

"*You* manage the house, Delia. *You* keep the accounts and make all the decisions." Lines creased the man's forehead. "It's a wonder you stay on."

"I promised your father I'd stay until......

There was along pause. "Until when?" he asked.

"Until your mother decides to move in with you. But that doesn't seem soon, does it?"

"No, it doesn't, and I don't know what we'd do without you, Delia Reardon. We owe you a great deal."

"No more than I owe your father. He was very good to me."

I was standing on the far side of the hall tree. Ellen's eyes were cast down as if she were inspecting the pattern on the rug. I wished there were something I could say, although of course there wasn't.

After they left, Delia looked up the front stairway and said, "That old lady is her own worst enemy and there isn't a thing anyone can do about it. We'll go into town now. No use ruining the rest of a lovely day."

∞

As we walked across the Common, I took notice of things to write home about. At the Deer Park, the animals peered through the fences at children calling in to them. We stopped to listen as a dark-skinned man wearing a red kerchief and a gold earring turned the handle of a music box. A small monkey collected coins in his tiny yellow hat.

"Is that man an Indian?" I asked in a whisper.

Delia smiled. "He's from Italy, and he's been working out in the sun all day. In the winter he'll be selling chestnuts."

My aunt continued pointing out the trees with signs in Latin, and the names of flowers and plants that I wouldn't be familiar with. I listened with interest, waiting for a chance to bring up the subject of Ballydare and Gran.

We were crossing a busy street, when a newsboy shouted the latest headline from a corner. He seemed to be doing a brisk business. "I think I'll write Gran and tell her how a boy could earn money in America," I said. "Edmund Burke says someday he wants to come here." When she didn't reply, I asked, "Did you know a family named Burke?"

"There were several with that name. None I knew well." She immediately pointed to a pigeon and suggested that on our way back we should buy peanuts and feed them.

It was clear to me that it was going to be even harder than I thought to introduce the subject of Ballydare or anyone in it for awhile. I would have to be patient.

Our first stop was the library, a red brick building with huge arched windows facing the Common. Its reading room was vast with high columns and leather chairs. A shabby old man, one shoe sole flapping on the gleaming tiles, carried a stack of books to a table and sat down across from a young man in a starched white collar. "Can *anyone* take out books?" I asked in a hushed tone, as if I were in a cathedral built for books.

"Anyone who can fill out a slip for a library card."

As I signed my name to request a card, I recalled that Delia said there were either two hundred thousand or two hundred and fifty thousand titles in this one building. If I never went to school another day, my name on this card would open more of the world to me than I would ever have met in Ballydare.

"I'll show you how to use the new card filing system," Delia said. "I prefer the old ledgers, but they'll soon be a thing of the past." She suggested a few titles, but I chose only one, *Uncle Tom's Cabin*, because I wanted an excuse to return as soon as possible.

From the library we strolled along Tremont Street, looking at the shop windows, then stopped at a tearoom for lunch. By the time we finished eating, a breeze had picked up. "It won't be long before you'll be needing a warm coat," Delia said as we entered the largest store I'd ever been in. My aunt cast a critical eye over several bolts of wool, and asked if there would be a better selection soon. She was assured there would be more choice in a week or so.

"You've never felt such cold as a Boston winter," she said as we walked toward the Public Garden.

"It couldn't be colder than the wind blowing across the Atlantic on Ballydare," I said. "Remember how cold that was? How good it felt coming inside to the turf fire." I looked over at her, wrapping my arms around my chest and pretending to shiver. Surely she couldn't ignore such a direct reminder.

"You've yet to feel a nor'easter, Mary," she said evenly as if I'd simply been referring to the weather anywhere. Would I never get her to respond?

Standing in line at the swan boats, I noticed that every adult had at least one child in tow, and guessed Delia was going on only because I was with her. We sat a few rows back from a young man who must have had strong legs to paddle the swan-shaped boat all day. As we glided along, with the swish of the paddle, the voices of the children calling out to turtles, it felt like we were on a miniature ocean, with each turtle-lined island a new land. I was about to say, "What stories Gran could have made up in a place like this!" when I looked toward the shore.

Tom Kerrigan was walking along the path with a young woman. He was dressed in a new suit and had had his haircut, but I knew it could only be Tom.

I jumped up from my seat and yelled, "Tom…Tom Kerrigan."

My aunt grabbed my sleeve and pulled me onto the wooden slatted seat with a thud. "For heaven's sake, Mary. Don't be yelling out like a fishwife. You're in a public place."

"But it's Tom Kerrigan. He was on the *Halcyon* with us. Theresa's been lighting candles to find him." I shouted again. "Tom. Tom,"

Delia said disapprovingly, "He seems to have found someone else soon enough."

"Maybe it's a friend…or someone's sister." I called "Tom," as loud as I could, and for a second I thought he heard me, but he turned back and spoke to the girl beside him.

"The breeze is carrying your voice away from him," Delia said, now looking intently at the couple.

The boat slipped around the far side of the island, and our view was cut off. By the time we'd circled the island with its family of ducks waddling along the edge, Tom and the girl were out of sight.

"Have you ever seen anyone so handsome in your life? I asked my aunt.

"Not for a long, long time," she answered quietly.

For the rest of the ride we didn't speak. As we stepped onto the platform filled with waiting children, I looked up and down the paths for Tom and the girl but there was no way to know which way they had gone.

Delia, who had been full of information about our surroundings earlier, now seemed a million miles away.

Walking home along Beacon Street, then turning up the hill, I told her how Tom and Theresa had spent all their time together, how she'd talked on into the night 'til I had to put my head under the pillow, and the way the crowd had listened to his songs.

"She says she'll never love anyone again after Tom," I stated with a sigh as we turned into Sabine Street. "It isn't as if Tom Kerrigan is just anyone, Aunt Delia. And there's little chance she'll find him in this big city, no matter how many candles she lights."

My aunt stopped on the brick path a moment, gazing at the trim bushes as if lost in thought. Then she said, "Don't say anything about seeing Tom today, Mary. It wouldn't be good to raise Theresa's hopes, but there may be a way to get in touch with him."

As soon as we entered the kitchen Marie Trottier said, "The old lady's been cross as a wet hen all day. Theresa's in her room, crying her eyes out or sulking." She lifted her own eyes toward the bell, as if she were directing her words to Edith Wooley's room. "I don't have to put up with her tongue, because Lady High-and-Mighty hasn't set foot in the kitchen in years. But I'll not send Cissy to take her abuse, no matter how long she rings that bell. I have only to drop a word after Mass and a dozen live-in-girls would spread the news that Marie Trottier's available." She slapped a thin cutlet into flour. "There's many a Boston family wishes I'd come cook for them. It would be under my own terms, too. Cissy and myself in the kitchen together."

"You and Cissy take off an extra day tomorrow, Marie," my aunt suggested. "I can manage."

"Thank you, Delia." Marie resumed dusting the thin slices, no longer slapping them. "I'll make up a fricassee this evening. It will be easily reheated."

"Don't bother," Delia said. "I can whip up something simple."

"I'm glad to do it. It's not you I'm angry with. It's her up there."

Theresa barely spoke that night, and she stayed to help Cissy with the dishes, as if she were putting off going to her room. I went straight upstairs to begin "*Uncle Tom's Cabin*". I'd read for less than an hour when Delia called me into her room. On the marble table beside her chair she'd set a china pot, covered with a cozy to keep the tea hot, two china cups and saucers, a glass dish with orange marmalade, another with butter, and a plate covered with a linen napkin..

"Hot from the oven, compliments of our sought after cook," she said, lifting the napkin, and filling the air with the aroma of fresh baked scones. "Sit down, Mary. There's something I want to show you."

She riffled through the pages of a newspaper, folded it open, and handed it to me. "Read the columns on the right hand side of the page."

My eyes ran down the long lists.

Ann and Mary Larkin seek news of Brothers, Cornelius and Bernard, arrived Boston, on the Lancaster, July, 1875. May have gone west. Write care of the Boston Pilot.

If anyone has heard from John Toomey, born county Clare, last address D Street, South Boston, 1870-72, contact following address.

Anyone knowing the whereabouts of Packy Riley will be handsomely rewarded.

On and on they went. Each a story in itself. Mothers, fathers, old neighbors, all looking for someone. Some dates reaching back for years.

When I looked up from the paper my aunt said, "More than one person may have noticed the handsome Tom Kerrigan by now. Perhaps he'll see the column himself, or at least have it pointed out to him.

I jumped up, ready to tell Theresa. "She can write, 'Theresa Noonan, recently arrived on the *Halcyon* seeks address of Thomas Kerrigan. Write to 48 Sabine Street, Boston.' "

"Not this address. Mrs. Wooley wouldn't appreciate it.

"Does she read *The Boston Pilot?*"

"A Catholic paper! Good heavens, no. She gets *The Transcript*. But there's another reason this address shouldn't be in the paper." Settling back in her chair, she filled our cups and took a few sips of tea. "Theresa shouldn't call attention to herself as a girl fresh off the boat. The docks are filled with men offering to carry bags, then running off with a girl's few possessions. Or a young man will follow after a girl, complimenting her on her fair skin, her beautiful eyes as if moonstruck. Then he'll tell her he knows a place with inexpensive lodgings. Though she may never before have sipped a drop of whiskey, he'll have her in a pub, and the innocent creature will be waking up in a… " She hesitated. "In a place of fallen women."

"But Theresa has a place to stay," I protested. "There'd be no danger now."

"Even after a girl is safely situated, she may be lonely and fall for a bit of flattery, given her because she has money in her pocket."

As my aunt's words rose and fell with the lilt of Ballydare, I wondered if she recognized the change in her voice. She surely didn't recognize herself in the stories she told. No man could have turned the head of a woman as smart as Delia Reardon. My heart continued to sink.

Finally, I asked, "How will Theresa find Tom if she can't write to him?"

"Theresa doesn't have to write the letter herself." Delia took a pen and sheet of paper from the back of the table. She scribbled a few lines, crossed them out, began over, then handed the note to me.

Tom Kerrigan, recently arrived on the Halcyon, can renew his acquaintance with shipboard companions, Mary and Theresa, by contacting Father Joseph Flynn at St. Joseph's Church, Boston."

I read the letter several times. It was wonderful idea. But I did ask, "Why did you put my name in with Theresa's?"

"Let him believe that you might have written it. If he doesn't answer, Theresa need never know, and we won't have embarrassed her." She took back the paper and folded it. "If he has good intentions, he'll not mind contacting a priest. Meanwhile, don't say anything. Nothing may come of the letter."

I picked up my book wishing I could immediately cheer Theresa. She would probably lie awake imagining more ghostly noises if she didn't have this new hope to fill her mind. When there was a bang and the curtains fluttered slightly, I almost dropped my book.

"Just a loose shutter banging in the wind," my aunt said.

As the white curtain continued to sway, I shivered. "It must get cold up here in the winter."

"It used to get bitter cold." Delia pointed to a small wooden chest beneath her window. "There's a register under it. Mr. Wooley had registers installed so heat could rise to these rooms. Not many living-in girls on the hill sleep in heated rooms. The next year, he had a toilet installed at the end of the hall."

I remembered the jolly looking man in the painting opposite the haughty Lady High-and-Mighty. "Why did such a nice man marry such a mean woman?" I asked.

"Because she was beautiful." Delia buttered another scone and spread a spoonful of marmalade over it. "Edith Wooley could talk pleasantly with a dinner companion, but I doubt she ever had an original thought in her head. It wasn't all that obvious until her daughter-in-law moved in."

Delia buttered a second scone for me. I guessed she was considering what to say next. I had never heard her say anything that could be considered gossip. If Mrs. Rafferty, in and out of dozens of laundry rooms and kitchens, shared news of scandalous behavior, my aunt left the room.

Finally, Delia said, "All her life, Edith Wooley had been the center of attention. Then here was this plain young woman who had both men and women listening to everything she said. And it wasn't as if Dorothy Wooley held the floor, letting no one else speak. She listened to others, with genuine interest."

That could be a description of Ellen, I thought, wanting to hear more.

"After Mr. Wooley died, the calling cards continued for awhile, but Edith Wooley ignored them and never returned a visit." She spread a bit of jam across her own second scone and sighed. "It's sad, but in a way it's not entirely her fault. Things had always come easily to her, and her husband spoiled her. When he lost an entire city block in the Boston Fire, he kept the newspapers out of the house so she wouldn't worry what the fire had cost him."

"She didn't know the city was on fire?"

"She *had* to know. Cissy and Marie saw horses rearing up in panic, as crowds ran toward the Common screaming. It was weeks before Cissy stopped trembling. That night the sky was bright for sixty miles as sixty acres of downtown Boston burned. A thousand business places were destroyed."

"When did it happen?"

"It was November,9, 1872. I remember the date because the

November the 9th is Pat's Birthday."

I sat forward in my chair. It was the first mention of anyone in Ireland. I was about to say Gran had knitted him a sweater for his birthday last November, but Delia didn't pause.

"The next year there was a financial panic. Insurance companies went bankrupt. The newspapers, both the Boston Glove and the Herald, had burned to the ground. Mr. Wooley lost a fortune.in investments, yet, Mrs. Wooley went on spending lavishly, because her husband never discussed finances with her."

As my aunt continued, telling the details of the dreadful fire as well as any shanachee or Gran, her voice became more Irish, and I could almost smell the smoke and see the night sky bright for miles and miles.

When I went back to my book, I couldn't concentrate. One minute I was picturing the quickly rebuilt streets of Boston that I had seen. Then I was remembering Pat and Aggie, counting coins at the end of each day. Discussing what they could afford next. Deciding together not to raise hens, because what would May Burke do if she couldn't sell a few eggs to Reardon's Store? And those thoughts brought me back to the extravagant Mrs. Wooley and the terrible fire in Boston.

In bed, with the rain and wind lashing against the windowpane, my own curtain swaying, I would be seeing rearing horses, flaming buildings, and screaming figures running toward the safety of the Common. I pulled the light blanket around my shoulders and replaced these images with the organ man and his monkey. The huge vault of the library reading room. Then Tom Kerrigan, walking out with someone other than Theresa.

A shutter rapped steadily, and the curtain continued to move. I turned my back and picked up my beads, saying the last decade for any poor girl the old lady might have driven into the streets with her sharp tongue. A girl who may have become a fallen woman, and her ghost come back to haunt 48 Sabine Street.

CHAPTER 19

It was hard not to tell Theresa about *The Boston Pilot*, since she was moping about so. To cheer her Mrs. Trottier prepared colcannon, a mixture of cabbage and potatoes, which Theresa claimed she missed terribly. "It's tasty," the cook said as she served it. "But it's not a dish I'd send upstairs."

That night, my aunt read aloud an article from *The Boston Pilot*. A Galway landlord had sent thirty families to America on a single ship, claiming the British government was taxing him so much for each tenant, that raising cattle was the only way he could keep going. She shook her head in disgust. "They've no idea in London what they're doing to Ireland. It's all columns and figures to them."

Finally, Delia had mentioned Ireland. I waited for her to go on, but she went back to the paper.

I returned to writing to my grandmother, finding it was easy once I'd started. I didn't need to say maid or housekeeper, only that I helped Delia by doing the dusting and polishing. In time, I would be more forthright. For now, because I really wanted to show my aunt in a favorable light, I quoted her comments on the English word for word.

The morning my aunt left to put the notice in the paper, she was carrying the same round box. As soon as she was gone, Theresa lightly touched my sleeve as I dusted and whispered, "I heard them again. Before dawn it was this time. Right over my bed."

"Well, I didn't hear a sound," I said. "It's probably those squirrels again."

"Squirrels don't move things around. They don't walk up and down the stairs. It's haunts, Mary." As her eyes widened with terror, I remembered Delia's keys.

"It's *not* haunts," I insisted." The dusting can wait. I'll get the key and go up into the attic with you right now. We'll likely find nuts all over the floor."

I went up the back staircase and went into my aunt's room. Her ring of keys were on the marble-topped table. I picked them up and went back into the hall where Theresa was waiting/

"You go first," Theresa said, standing aside when I'd unlocked the attic door.

"No, it's you who needs to see there's no haunt up there. I'm not the one afraid," I protested, although I dreaded the thought of cobwebs brushing against my face.

Reluctantly, Theresa took a cautious step up the narrow stairway. Then another. I followed closely, relieved that she would have swept away any cobwebs. She stopped on each tread to draw in a breath of dry air that smelled like the storeroom behind Reardon's Store.

"Hurry up, Theresa, we can't be taking all day," I said, feeling a sneeze coming on. "For all you know, the bell is ringing in the kitchen, and no one has any idea where you are."

A few steps from the top she screamed, and backed down almost on top of me. By the time we were at the bottom, I was shivering as much as she was. Pale as any ghost, her voice quivering, she said, "Dead people, Mary. The attic is full of them."

I swallowed the lump rising in my throat. "You couldn't have seen dead people. Maybe it was a sheet or a curtain moving."

"It was *dead* people I saw, Mary. Dead ladies in hats, like they'd come to some fancy tea at the Big House." She pushed past me, and I followed her into her room and sat next to her on the edge of her bed. She gripped a bottle of holy water so tight her knuckles were white. "I can't sleep another night under this roof I'd not dare close my eyes. . I'm leaving"

My mind was spinning. Dead people in the attic. Ghosts in hats, gathered for tea. It was ridiculous. But other maids had slept in Theresa's room and left. Had they fled because they'd heard the same noises? But the thought of Theresa out on the street, after what my aunt had said about the dangers in the city was too awful to accept.

In a voice calmer than I was feeling, I said, "I'll go first this time and you follow."

"Not me." She held out the bottle of holy water. "Sprinkle this as you go."

"But you have to come behind me. It's only fair."

"I'll stand at the foot, saying prayers for you."

I knew that was the best she was going to offer. I took the holy water. My knees shaking, I made a sign of the cross and sprinkled holy water on each step, adding a few extra drops at every creak.

Three quarters of the way up, I stood still, and peered into the wan light above. I knew no special prayer to guard against ghosts, which I promptly told myself were not there anyway, but said a quick Hail Mary for protection and courage. With my heart pounding I took the final steps.

I never had a prayer answered so quickly in my life!

Four dressmaker's forms loomed in the center of the room covered in sheets. I recognized what they were because Aggie kept one in the storeroom. in the back of the store. On a shelf directly behind them, oval forms held hats like the sort Delia wore. As my eyes adjusted to the light from the gable windows, I saw two long tables, one with pieces of cloth and ribbons, the other held at least a dozen vases filled with feathers of different sizes and colors.

I knew at once. Delia made hats. And Delia sold hats.

The haunts and ghostly sounds, had been Delia moving around in the attic. Every time Theresa complained, Delia had gone out with a hat box that morning.

"Come on up," I called over my shoulder. "There's nothing to be afraid of." There was no answer. Assuming Theresa hadn't waited as she'd promised, I walked toward the tables. When the floorboard creaked, I stopped to take my bearings. I was probably directly over Theresa's bed. The only cobwebs were in the corners of the attic. On the nearer table, I recognized the gray braid on the hat my aunt wore to the dock. Among the feathers on the second table a single jet black plume rose from a narrow vase. As I wondered what strange bird it had come from, I heard footsteps on the stairs.

"Come see your ghosts," I called again "They're only dress making forms and feathers."

But it was not Theresa who stepped over the threshold. "How did you get up here?" my aunt demanded. "The attic is kept locked."

Flustered, I explained, "Theresa thought she heard ghosts, and said she couldn't sleep another night in this house." In the dim light I couldn't see my aunt's expression. "I borrowed your keys so she wouldn't run off."

As Delia walked forward into the light from the windows, I saw she was more embarrassed than angry. She took off a hat very much like the one on the nearest form and laid it next to a vase of white plumes. "Designing hats is something I like to do, now and then," she said. "I make a few dollars, selling them to the big stores. From time to time, I'll see them on the most fashionable women in Boston."

"They're beautiful," I said. "You should open a hat store."

"I barely made enough to keep me alive, working for a milliner for a year."

"But *designing* hats like these is different from working on *ordinary* hats. You could have owned your own business."

My aunt looked at me with a somewhat sad smile. "Mary, I came to America at the wrong time for an Irish girl to choose what she wanted to do. With you it will be different. You'll find what you're best at. What you truly want to do with your life." Her smile broadened. "I suspect you aren't setting your sights on a grand house in need of constant dusting and polishing."

She went to the gable and lifted the narrow window. A waft of fresh air streamed into the dusty attic. Then she sat on a horsehair chair with a ripped arm, and told me to sit opposite in a cane rocker. Sunlight fell across her face revealing fine lines around her eyes I hadn't noticed before.

For the next hour, high above the road, up where the small top leaves of the maple tree were turning red and gold, and dust danced in the shifting sunbeams, Aunt Delia told how she had learned of my parents' death in a column devoted to news from Galway. I leaned forward in my rocker taking in every word as she described how my mother had followed her around the house, sat on her lap, and spoken her first words to her.

"She spoke clearly from the start. But we called her "Baby" so often that's how she referred to herself."

"She called you Delie, didn't she?" I said when she paused for a moment.

She looked at me in surprise. "She did. And who told you that?"

"Uncle Pat. The day before I left. He said she cried for "her Delie" for weeks."

My aunt bit her bottom lip and looked down at the floor. Then she sat up straight, her hands gripping the arms of the chair. "Mary, I'll see that you receive an education that would make your mother proud. You'll not keep house, or dust, or polish, unless it's for yourself and your own family. You won't be rushing into marriage to get out from under the thumb of some employer like Edith Wooley. You'll be anything you want to be."

As she continued, her promises became a challenge. I had no idea what I wanted to be. And I doubted anyone could live up to Baby Mary Ellen, the perfect little girl with the sunny smile and loving nature everyone remembered.

Delia Reardon laid out my future, her face becoming more and more animated. "A new school has opened. Girls Latin School promises to give as fine an education as Boys Latin School which prepares boys for Harvard."

She was expecting too much of me. I was clever at learning, but I'd seldom had to study. Often my mind had wandered as the teacher droned on in the little classroom of Ballydare. And there was so much I didn't know. On the Common, I'd taken the organ grinder for an Indian. I'd been surprised to learn New York was not only a city, but a state. How would I fare among students who'd been in Boston schools all their lives? Who had had library cards from the time they could read?

Girls Latin School. The name gave me visions of girls brushing past me, speaking to each other in a strange language. I didn't know any Latin, except *dominus vobiscum and et cum spiritu tuo* from the Mass. And Ave Maria was the same as saying Hail Mary.

By the time she told me that the daughter of the editor of *The Woman's Journal* attended Boston University I realized that from the day I arrived, my aunt had been looking for my strong points, crossing off my weaknesses, to send me in the direction I would do best. And as she leaned toward me, her palms turned upward, I felt she was offering me the life my mother hadn't lived to see. The life she might have chosen for herself if there had been no famine.

A great sense of relief swept over me. I no longer had to avoid writing to Gran about being a maid in a house where Delia was the housekeeper. When Gran learned how generous her daughter was, working and saving all those years, then spending extra so we could cross the ocean in cabin class, Gran would write to Delia. Delia would write back.

For another ten minutes as my aunt Delia talked and I listened, I wondered if I could possibly live up to the future she was offering me.

It was a relief to leave the attic and return to the rooms below where all I had to face was dusting and polishing and trimming lamps.

CHAPTER 20

I thought Marie Trottier was only teaching me a few words of French, but as we peeled potatoes she made me repeat several times, "J'aime les pommes de terre. Aussi, J'aime les carrottes,"and corrected the way I pronounced the rs. I knew then that Aunt Delia had asked her to teach me the language.

"I feel silly trying to say it that way," I protested.

"Marcel, my husband, insisted I pronounce each word correctly from the beginning. 'You'll thank me someday', he'd say. 'You never know what the future holds in store.'" She checked the oven where a loaf of bread was showing the first tinges of golden brown, and returned to the table. "Marcel never let on that he didn't expect to live long. He became a tyrant in the kitchen, making me get the sauces right, take the vegetables off while still crisp. I wouldn't be where I am today if he hadn't prepared me so well. The winter Marcel died was the hardest of my life."

The difficulties of learning French were often mixed with descriptions of how alone Marie Trottier had felt, with Sissy sickly through those long cold months in Quebec. On Good Friday, when a few crocuses had barely pushed through the snow, she decided to leave.

"I sold the house. There was nothing for me back in Ireland, so I came to Boston. I asked the priest what paper the rich families read and put an advertisement in *The Transcript*." A smile flickered across her face. "But I didn't present myself an Irish woman who could cook."

"What did you say in the advertisement?" I asked wishing I could tell her about the notice we'd put in *The Pilot* for Theresa.

She closed her eyes and said, as if she were reading, *Madame Trottier, trained in the art of French cuisine by master chef of Paris and Quebec, is available to cook for family of refined tastes.* A week later I was working for the Lodges on Beacon Street. The Wooleys came for dinner several times and offered me twice the wages. I made it clear that Cissy would come with me, gave my notice, and have been here ever since."

"Was my aunt the housekeeper then?"

"She was the upstairs maid. But she was so smart, suggesting ways to save money, how to keep the girls from leaving when they'd have a run in with the old lady, I knew in time she'd be housekeeper." Marie opened the oven, tapped the brown crusts, and set the loaves on a rack to cool. "Eventually your aunt had the old gentleman paying Cissy for working here in the kitchen. She even helped me make provisions for Cissy if anything happened to me."

"How did she manage that?" I asked, more amazed than ever by my aunt's abilities.

"She'd been buying up a few properties, here and there, and advised me to take some of the money from selling the Quebec house and buy the empty lot next to the House of the Angel Guardian. Someday the sisters would have to expand. Then she and I went to the Bishop, and said the lot would go to the convent if he could persuade the Mother Superior to find a place in the kitchen for Cissy, in the event of my death. Cissy visits the sisters every few months, and they're fond of her. Believe me, it's a load off my mind knowing she'll be safe and happy there."

I was thinking that no one in Ballydare would dare to make a suggestion to a bishop or Mother Superior, when Delia came into the kitchen. She handed a slim envelope to Theresa, a thicker one to me, and left. My heart leapt. The stamps were from Ireland. I shuffled through the pages and found there were several letters.

Gran's handwriting was shakier than I remembered it. She said she was fine and it was a good thing she could be helping out, "as Aggie's time grew near". She asked if I'd made friends in my new school, and ended saying Father Sheehy asked about me every Sunday and that when I wrote to him I should address the envelope to The Reverend Joseph F. X. Sheehy. Inside I could simply call him Father Sheehy. She did not ask about Delia.

In large, bold handwriting, Aggie had written that it was good Gran had moved in with them. With the weather so cold and damp, my grandmother's rheumatism was acting up. She hoped I was happy, and that my aunt Delia was becoming as fond of me as she and my uncle Pat were. She ended with a flourish. "But how could she fail to love such a wonderful niece? Love from both of us, Aunt Aggie and Uncle Pat."

Maggie wrote that her mother had made her three new dresses for school. This year arithmetic was her favorite subject. She was now best friends with Mary Claire Mahoney, and no longer liked Mary Frances Rooney.

Jamesy's half a page, I guessed, was written at the insistence of his parents. School was fine. The weather was fine. He felt fine. I hope you are fine. Your Cousin, James A. Reardon

Lizzie sent a crayon drawing of a house with smoke coming out the chimney, a cat sitting in front that was almost as big as the house, and LZIZLE scrawled across the bottom.

Two pages, cut from a brown paper bag, were folded and sealed with drippings of candle wax. I pulled my chair close to the window to read the smudged lines of Edmund's pencil.

Dear Mary,

I am happy to know that Boston is such an interesting place. Your grandmother told me about the wonderful library there. I wish we had such a grand library in Ballydare, because I have not been going to school much lately.

Please do not mention this in any letters you send home. I will be leaving school once the weather turns bad. My mother needs me with her most of the time, as she's haunted more and more by the famine days. Sometimes she is quite herself, but she forgets she was the only one who survived, and goes searching for her family. I'm afraid in the winter, she will come to harm. People don't know how sick she is getting, because I find her pretty quickly and get her home.

Mary, is there a chance I could earn a living in America? Maybe if she is away from the sights and memories, her mind will not be so troubled. I have grown almost two inches since spring and think I can pass for fourteen. I am willing to do anything.

Please don't tell anyone I asked you these questions.

Your friend,

Edmund Burke

I sat cross-legged on the bed, remembering. Edmund, running barefoot up the road to sit with Gram and me at the story stone. His mother, waiting in the doorway on the first day of school until he'd walked over, patted her hand, and gone back to his seat. The bitterness in his voice as he'd said, "I'm Father Sheehy's altar boy. I'm not supposed to hate anyone, but I understand the people who do."

Edmund Burke had been a grownup most of his life. But could he earn a living in America for the two of them? Even if he had a good corner for selling newspapers, would he, with his gentle nature, be the sort that Mrs. Moriarty said were beaten up by hooligans?

I was reading his letter again when Delia tapped on the door and opened it. "You should be downstairs to eat." She turned white as she saw the letter in my hand, the tears I was wiping from my eyes. "What's happened? Has my mother-?"

"Gran's fine, except her rheumatism is acting up."

"Pat?"

"Pat is fine, too, and Aunt Aggie." When I held out Gran's letter, she turned and left the room as if no news of anyone in Ireland held the least bit of interest for her.

But I had seen her expression and I knew better. *Delia cared.*

CHAPTER 21

I dropped my prayers that the English be expelled from Ireland forever. There were enough people in Ireland praying for that. The first decade of the rosary became a request that Mae Burke would get well, and Edmund be able to stay in school.

I would put off writing to Edmund until I could offer some good suggestions. Boys his age didn't just sell newspapers. They ran errands for shopkeepers. Shook down burnt coals in furnaces, then hauled out the ashes in the back alleys. But on the nickels and dimes they earned, I doubted they were supporting their families. And wouldn't his mother be even worse off, roaming among the high buildings of Boston, with never a familiar hand to lead her home?

Poor Edmund I thought, and stopped. I would not call him that. Ever. It was unlucky.

∞

A few days later I received a letter with an American stamp. My first thought was that Mrs. Moriarty had read *The Pilot* and tracked us down through St. Joseph's Church. I opened it as my aunt looked on. Glancing at the signature, I exclaimed, "It's from Ellen Wooley!"

Delia looked as surprised as I felt. "What in the world?"

I scanned the page and read aloud.

Dear Mary,

There are some books in the bottom dresser drawer of my old room that are not considered "literature" by teachers or by my mother, but I loved them. They are about poor boys who make their way in the world by pluck and luck. Please let me know what you think of them.

With great hopes that you will like America,
Ellen Wooley

"Ellen's room was next to the nursery on the third floor. Run right up and get the books," my aunt said. I knew she was pleased. She called after me, "You must write back and thank Ellen immediately."

I had never been in the rooms on the third floor, and knew only that they were dusted and aired once a week. Cold air filled the narrow hallway as I passed a large room. Theresa was shaking a scatter rug out the window.

"My aunt will get after you for doing that," I called in. "You're supposed to take the carpet beater to them outside in the back."

"There's no dirt in them, anyway. Why anyone should be cleaning a room that's not used, I can't for the life of me see." She closed the window and swept her arm around. "Have you ever seen such toys, Mary? They must have cost a fortune."

She led me past a wooden horse on rockers and an iron train big enough for a small child to sit on, and picked up a monkey dressed in a tiny red coat and hat. "Little Mikey would love this," she said wistfully, moving the jointed arms and legs. When she turned a key in the back, we were surprised by a tinkling song like the hurdy gurdy on the Common. "If I could find one, I'd send it to him, even if it took a week's wages." Her face clouded as she slumped onto the edge of a bed. "Instead, I have to send money, so Paddy can have shoes for school. His old ones are through at the soles."

I had forgotten the letter she'd received the same day I had. "Was there much news from home, Theresa?"

"Just the same old thing. My mother does her best, and I don't begrudge a few dollars, but I'll need a warm coat myself. No one here goes to church in a shawl except the old women."

Delia had brought home a length of heavy wool, and was already cutting out a coat for me. "You can use my white shawl 'til you get your coat," I offered. "It doesn't look like what the old women wear." I left her staring down at the monkey in her hands.

Entering Ellen's room was like stepping into a garden. The wallpaper was trellised with tiny climbing roses. A mirrored dresser caught the afternoon sun. I crossed the flowered carpet and pulled open the bottom drawer. In the back, I found half a dozen books by the same author. Every cover showed a shabby boy with a pleasant, but determined look, reminding me of Edmund Burke.

I gathered them in my apron, and placed them in the back of my own bureau drawer to read after my hour with the American history book my aunt had assigned to me.

As we sat in Delia's room that night, with our usual cups of tea and toast and jam, she asked, "Will Ellen's books be useful for your studies, Mary?"

I hesitated "They're not school books. They're American stories."

"By James Fennimore Cooper? Louisa May Alcott?"

"They're by a man named Horatio Alger."

Delia set down her teacup. "Horatio Alger! I'm surprised Ellen's mother would let her waste her time on penny dreadfuls."

"Penny dreadfuls?" The very words sounded exciting.

"Cheap novels about poor boys on the street, or set in the wild west with Indians. Cowboys."

I didn't say it, but I thought penny dreadfuls sounded more interesting than the history of the Massachusetts Bay Colony in my hand.

At the end of an hour, I yawned several times and my aunt told me to go to bed. An hour later as I sat up in bed with an extra blanket around my shoulders, she called in, "Put down Horatio Alger and go to sleep, Mary."

I snuffed out the oil lamp, and leaving *Phil the Fiddler* hungry on the streets of New York, I picked up my rosary, but fell asleep somewhere in the middle.

CHAPTER 22

Morning frost coated the grass and bushes as we walked to St. Joseph's. My warm winter coat fit perfectly. Aggie would have insisted, on leaving room to grow. When I mentioned that Theresa had come back from early Mass chilled, Delia said, "She squanders her wages on frills. She should think ahead."

"She doesn't just squander it. She sends money home."

My aunt looked surprised. "Does she, now?" was her only comment.

But that evening as she inspected an old coat of her own my aunt said, "If I turn the material, it will be good as new. Get Theresa so I can take her measurements."

I thought the color, gray as the slate on the roof, dreary, until three days later Delia added a light gray tippet of fur, and two inches of black braid on the sleeves. "With a becoming hat, you'll look as if you stepped out of *Godey's Ladies Book*," she said,

When my aunt held swatches of velvet, and braid up to Theresa's face and hair, I put my book aside. Delia was humming as her fingers flew.

Too bad she can't be doing this all the time, I thought. Even if she did have some gray hair and fine lines around her eyes, I could see her opening a hat shop.

∞

Although the next Sunday was warm, Theresa wore the coat to

church. I wore only my blue dress. "Indian summer," Delia said as we walked back. "We'll have a few lovely days before the winter sets in."

Indian summer. I loved the sound of it, as well as the picture of Indians around a fire eating ears of corn, which I'd tasted for the first time a week before.

We'd barely entered the house when Mrs.Trottier rushed from the kitchen. "Something's wrong with Mrs. Wooley," she said in the tone of awe used around the worst of news. "You'd better get the doctor."

"It wasn't my fault," Theresa sputtered. "I was straightening up and she got into a state and suddenly …"

My aunt raced up the stairs. In less than a minute she came down holding onto the railing. "I'll get Dr. Dudley. He's only two streets away." As Delia left, I realized it was the only time I'd seen her go out of the house without gloves.

Marie, Cissy, Theresa and I listened to the ticking of the kitchen clock. Then the chimes sounded the quarter hour in the parlor. At the half hour, my aunt and the doctor came in and went straight upstairs. Fifteen minutes later, we heard muffled words in the hall. Marie took out her rosary.

"Maybe she died," Cissy whispered, making the sign of the cross.

I sat silently, ashamed that when Cissy said, "Maybe she died." my first thought had not been about Mrs. Wooley, but that now we could leave Sabine Street. I felt so guilty, I'd have gone to confession on the spot if Father Sheehy had been there, knowing he must have heard even worst thoughts about rent collectors, landlords, and the English government.

The clock was chiming the hour when Delia told us, "Mrs. Wooley may have had a mild stroke. Her speech is slurred and she hasn't full use of her left side. Dr. Dudley will send a telegram to her son, and come by in the morning."

"I didn't do anything wrong. I was only rearranging-"

Delia cut in, "No one is blaming you, Theresa. But it's better if I stay with her. Lord knows I've been here long enough for her to be used to me."

For the rest of the day every sound was magnified. Cissy dropped a cup in the pantry and we jumped. Two cats snarled and hissed in the back alley and a shiver ran through my body. On the way up to bed, Theresa whispered, "I don't know what's to become of us, Mary."

In her room we knelt beside her bed to say a prayer for the repose of Mrs. Wooley's soul.

That night my aunt slept on the same floor with Mrs. Wooley. I lay awake listening to chestnuts drop onto the sidewalk across the street, trying to think of one good thing about Edith Wooley.

∞

The next morning, Doctor Dudley told my aunt, "Mrs. Wooley's speech is still slurred, but it's improving. Her son sent word that he and his wife will drop by this morning. I'll be at the hospital until one o'clock, but they can talk with me after that."

"Shouldn't she be kept from anything upsetting?" Delia asked.

The doctor coughed slightly. "I'm aware there's a bit of tension, but her daughter-in-law wants to come. I hope her son can get her to change her mind.

When George Wooley arrived, his wife was not with him. Ellen stepped out of the carriage and gazed up at the window to her grandmother's room, until her father took her hand. They came in and went straight upstairs.

A few minutes later, Delia came to the kitchen door. "A pitcher of lemonade, and a few cookies, Marie," she said, then turned to me. "Carry the tray into the parlor and sit and talk with Ellen. I'm afraid she'll burst into tears if she remains upstairs."

Ellen was in the wingback chair facing her grandmother's portrait when I came in. I set the tray on a small table in front of her, and sat stiffly on a carved chair opposite with my hands folded on my lap. Finally I said, "Dr. Dudley believes your Grandmother is already improving."

Ellen broke off the edge of a lemon crisp. Since Marie had placed two glasses on the tray, I took one and slipped slowly, wondering what I could say to fill the awkward silence. We had both witnessed her Grandmother's behavior toward Andrew when he'd dropped the porcelain dog.

"My mother wanted to come, but my father said it might do more harm than good," Ellen said." She bit her lip as if she didn't want to go on, but then added almost in a rush, "My grandmother wasn't always as cranky as she is now. When I was little she used to let me look through her jewelry boxes, and she'd tell me where each piece came from. But in May-"

She wiped a tear from her cheek and took a deep breath. "In May she told my father she was glad she had a granddaughter to leave her jewelry to, because my mother was not to get a thing belonging to her. They'd had the most ridiculous argument. Grandmother said women didn't need to vote because a wife would always vote the way her husband did, and if she weren't clever enough to have caught a husband, she wasn't smart enough to vote anyway. My mother got really angry and snapped back, "There are plenty of married women without a brain in their heads." Ellen sniffled and managed a small smile. "Sometimes I wish my mother wouldn't talk so much about those things, but she can't seem to help it, any more than Grandma can keep from ridiculing what she calls my mother's "foolish notions." When we moved out, my father said the Chinese character for trouble is two women under one roof."

"I hope that's not true," I said. "My grandmother went to live with my Aunt Aggie. But Gran calls Aggie the "peacemaker in the family."

"My father tries to make peace, but he can't please them both. I don't think he ever will."

As we drank the lemonade, to take her mind off her mother and grandmother, I told her about Mrs. Moriarty, and then Theresa and Tom, doing almost all the talking until her father and my aunt came down stairs.

"You'll need to hire more help, Delia," George Wooley suggested as soon as he came into the room.

"We can manage as we are," Delia said. "It might be hard right now to break someone in."

"I'll stop by tomorrow, then." He laid his hand on his daughters arm. "If your grandmother is feeling better, you can come back on Saturday."

Ellen nodded and followed her father. But on the threshold of the parlor she looked back for a moment at the portrait of her grandmother as a young girl, with an expression of sympathy. An expression I couldn't imagine on the beautiful girl above the mantle, even less on the handsome woman in the next room wearing diamonds.

∞

Mrs. Trottier had just prepared a cup of broth for Mrs. Wooley when the brass knocker sounded against the front door. "Everything comes in threes," she said. "Weeks go by with no one at the front, now here's the third time in two days. You answer it, Theresa. Miss Reardon has her hands full. Mary, you carry the tray upstairs."

Theresa paused at the hall tree mirror to smooth her apron and tuck in any stray hair, as if opening the door were a step above making beds and dusting. I'd gone halfway up the stairs when I heard a cry, between a squeal and a shriek. I almost dropped the tray.

"What in the world is going on?" my aunt called, as she came down from the second floor.

"It's Tom. Tom Kerrigan," I said softly. "He must have read *The Pilot.*"

Tom Kerrigan stood in the center of the hall with Theresa clinging to his arm. I couldn't tell whether my aunt was staring or gazing at him. It was almost half a minute before she said crisply, "Fortunately, the lady of the house is sleeping or she'd have your head for calling at the front door, young man. Next time, come to the servants' entrance at the side."

Tom turned to me. "Is your aunt ill, that she's sleeping in the middle of the day, Mary?
I didn't mean to create such a stir."

I nodded toward Delia. "That was my aunt speaking. She's the housekeeper. Me and Theresa work…"

"Theresa and I," Delia corrected.

Embarrassed by Delia's tone, I added quickly, "It's my aunt who put the notice in *The Pilot*. And kept it running all this time."

"Oh, Miss Reardon," Theresa burst out. "I never expected you'd do such a kind-"

"Well, I did, and as you certainly won't have your mind on much around here, you may as well take the rest of the day off. Tom can wait in the kitchen while you change."

As she turned, Tom called after her, "Miss Reardon, thank you for your kindness. You say the lady of the house is sleeping, but, sure there's no grander lady in this house than yourself."

When Delia looked back over her shoulder, I wondered if I were the only one who thought her eyes were glistening.

Theresa left, wearing the green dress under her new coat. Mrs. Trottier said, "They make a handsome couple, don't they?"

The laundress, Mrs. Rafferty, shook her head. "Handsome they may be, but I've ironed enough shirts to recognize one that cost a fortune. Hardly in the country, and he's dressing like a dandy. I hope he's not into something shady."

Cissy gasped and her mother replied, "It's a great fault you have, Peggy Rafferty, passing judgments so quickly."

At the word "dandy" I remembered Mrs. Moriarty's comment. "A real crowd pleaser that young man is. Dandy'll have him singing at meetings, stirring up the crowd. He'll go far in politics." I suspected Dandy O'Connor had already started Tom in that direction. And Tom *would* surely be a crowd pleaser. He had even managed to please Aunt Delia.

That night as I read in my own room I found it hard to keep my mind on my book. Delia Reardon was such a contradiction. She had been abrupt with Tom, then given Theresa the rest of the day off to be with him. After complaining that Theresa squandered money, she'd made her a coat. When Tom called up the stairs with a compliment, it was as if she'd been caught completely off-guard.

On the swan boat when I'd asked if she'd ever seen anyone so handsome, she'd replied, "Not in a long, long time." Had Delia once loved someone as handsome and charming as Tom? Was it in America, or in Ballydare? Soon I was imagining a young Delia, looking something like me, being courted by a dashing young man. I made him lighter haired than Tom , and as nice as Edmund But there had to have been a great problem. He could have been protestant, even English, and even though he swore to convert and raise the children in the one true faith, the families were opposed. (I had already read halfway through *Romeo and Juliet*.)

Then I recalled the terrible blowup Uncle Pat had witnessed. Gran's never wanting me to go near Ashmont. Because I couldn't imagine that my grandmother would ever have stopped the course of true love, I picked up *Ragged Dick* and spent the rest of the evening reading.

On Saturday afternoon Ellen Wooley came with her father. She stayed an hour with her Grandmother, then came downstairs and asked me to go to the attic with her. "We left in such a hurry, I shoved school books and things into boxes," she explained as we climbed the narrow stairs . "You may be able to use them. That is if you would like them."

"I'd be glad to have them," I said, sneezing as we entered the dusty attic.

Ellen looked around at the long tables and feather-filled vases "I used to wonder why your aunt went out with hat boxes so often, until one day I found a skeleton key and came up to the attic. Later, I recognized the hats on Mrs. Dana and Miss Longwood as they came out of church."

"Someday she's going to open a hat shop," I regretted the comment as Ellen's face fell.

"She isn't thinking of leaving, is she?"

"Not while your grandmother is sick, and Mrs. Trottier and Cissy will stay as long as my aunt does."

Looking relieved, Ellen reached into the dark area under the eaves and pulled out a wooden box, crammed with magazines. "The last *Saint Nicholas Magazine* has a story by Louisa May Alcott. Even the old Woman's Journals can be interesting." She brushed a lock of hair back and sat on the floor beside the box. "Mary, we didn't expect to move out as quickly as we did. It all happened very fast. My father hopes someday my grandmother will come to live with us. But she's still angry with my mother, so it won't happen for a long time."

"You needn't worry about any of us leaving for awhile," I replied, little guessing how soon my words would be proven false.

CHAPTER 23

The next week, hearing a din louder than thunder, I ran into the kitchen still carrying the feather duster. "That's coal going down the chute," Mrs. Trottier explained. "You'll be glad you're in a house with a furnace that heats every room."

When I stepped out the front door, the smoke rising from every chimney filled the air with a sharper smell than burning turf. As light snow settled on my hair and shoulders, I thought of the times I'd run out to catch flakes on my tongue, Gran coming after me with a shawl and a warning. "You'll be down with a fever if you don't get back inside."

I hadn't heard from Ireland in three weeks. Were they waiting to write when Aunt Aggie had the baby?

Cissy was knitting long strips that Marie would stitch together as a baby blanket, and I was tempted to take a few coins from the money I'd hidden to buy a present. Gran had always let me keep some of the goose egg money to spend and put in the basket at church. I would ask Delia for some of the money she set aside for me out of my wages.

My aunt was back in her own room, because George Wooley had insisted she hire a girl whose only task was to wait on his mother. That night as we finished a pot of lukewarm tea, to introduce my need for money, I told her about Cissy's blanket, adding "She's also planning to knit Tom a scarf for Christmas. Mrs. Trottier gives Cissy some of her wages so she can buy yarn and little things she finds when they go to town." I set my cup and saucer on the low table between us. "Don't you agree that every woman should have a purse of her own?"

Delia put her book aside. "A purse of her own! Good heavens, Mary, what have you been reading?"

"The Woman's Journal. They were in the attic, and Ellen said I'd find them interesting."

My aunt shook her head. "You should be saving your money. I give you a coin each Sunday for church. I can make your clothing for a fraction of what they would cost to buy."

" It's Christmas presents I'm wanting to buy."

Delia looked at me over the rim of her glasses. "Remember, the money would be coming out of your savings where you're earning interest." I must have looked bewildered. "Banks pay to use money, Mary. Mrs. Wooley lives on the interest the bank pays her. The really rich live on the interest of their interest."

I gasped at the idea of people being that rich. Delia continued. "As to the article, well-to-do women may write that every woman needs a purse of their own, and still pay their servants a pittance. They'll have them at their beck and call from dawn 'til midnight, then look down on them for never making something of themselves. For all their advanced notions, they have no idea that they live in a different world from most people." She poured the last of the cold tea into her cup. After a few sips she said, "Let your money work for you. You can be generous with presents, but money makes money if you know what to do with it."

She got up, pulled out a dresser drawer, and drew out a stack of envelopes. Taking a one-dollar bill from each, she handed me ten dollars. "From now on, you'll be getting a dollar a week. The rest must go into the bank."

Overwhelmed to have ten dollars in my hand, for the rest of the evening I absentmindedly turned pages, thinking about the presents I could send to Ireland.

The announcement was a single sheet in Gran's handwriting.

Dear Mary,

Aggie had twin boys, Vincent Thomas, and Francis

Edward. Beautiful babies they are, but they don't give their mother a moment's rest. It's a blessing she has me here with an extra pair of arms to hold one baby while the other is being tended to. I will write a longer letter next time I want this to catch the mail.

Love from all of us,
Gran

Imagining Reardon's house and store, babies crying, neighbors dropping by, the bell jangling as customers came and went, I wondered if Gran sometimes missed the peace and quiet of the cottage. I read the letter to Delia. She smiled, which I thought showed some progress, but asked no questions.

∞

With Jean Cameron tending to Mrs. Wooley, Delia and I went shopping on a blustery cold day, with a sea wind tunneling between the high buildings. I found matching bibs for Vincent and Francis. A bottle of lily of the valley toilette water for Aggie The salesclerk recommended a select blend of pipe tobacco for Uncle Pat, and for James and Maggie, one hundred glass marbles with swirls of red, white, and blue at the bargain price of fifty cents because they were left over from the centennial celebration. I was pleased to recognize the date from my history reading.

I wanted something for Gran that only I could give her. On our way down Tremont Street, I stopped and gazed at a display of carefully posed family pictures. Delia placed her hand on my shoulder. "Belcher is considered the finest photographer in Boston. Your grandmother would love a picture of you."

We went down a narrow hall to a windowless room. As the photographer led me to an ornately carved chair in front of a plain backdrop, in the firmest voice I could muster, I said, "This is for our family in Ireland. I'd like us both to be in it."

Delia's hand flew toward her hat as if she'd been struck by a blast of wind. "I am not dressed for a photograph. Your dress is fine."

"But I want them all to see my new coat. You can wear your hat and coat as if we're outside.' Flustered, Delia looked around at the family portraits arranged along the wall. The photographer, obviously afraid he was going to lose a customer, spoke up. "I've a bench and backdrop that will look as if you are in the open air."

After he'd set up his equipment, he told me to sit down. When he said, "If you'll sit a bit straighter younger lady, and fold your hands in your lap." I immediately pulled my shoulders back and held my head higher. The photographer smiled and turned to Delia. "Now, Madame, if you'll place your hand on your daughter's shoulder and lean slightly toward her, the portrait will be more natural."

He disappeared behind the black curtain covering his camera. We held our poses for what seemed ages through flash after flash. I tried not to move, but Delia's hand on my shoulder trembled the entire time.

CHAPTER 24

When I asked if I could go shopping with Cissy, my aunt agreed. I knew she guessed I wanted to buy her present. The day was blustery and we didn't cross through the Common but went straight toward the stores.

At the busy corner of Park Street and Tremont, the newsboy I had usually glimpsed from a distance was shivering in a coat that barely closed. When we were closer, I saw the bluish-brown of what looked like a fading black eye, and hoped he hadn't been the victim of one of the "hooligans" Mrs. Moriarty had warned Ned Kelley about.

Cissy picked out a skein of pale green yarn in Hovey's and I found a nicely shaped scent bottle for Delia in a smaller store. On the way home as we bought roasted chestnuts on the Common, I noticed four boys furtively glancing toward the newsboy. Two held sticks. Two rocks the size of their fists. As they started toward his corner, I whispered, "Cissy, you tell the policeman over by the statue some boys may be planning to attack the boy selling newspapers. I'll warn the newsboy that they're coming with sticks and rocks."

She held on to my sleeve. "Mama says, never, never, go near where there's fighting. It's dangerous."

I pulled away. "They won't go after him unless he's alone. Please, go tell the policeman."

I walked quickly as if I was going to buy a paper. The boys

with sticks and rocks hung back. As I handed over two cents, I said in a low voice, "Four boys are watching you holding rocks and sticks, but my friend is telling the policeman."

The boy snarled, "Let 'em come. They ain't takin' the best corner in Boston from me."

"But you can't fight off four of them."

He slipped a scarred hand into a pocket and drew out a knife. Only his quivering lip showed that he wasn't as tough as he was pretending to be.

"Put that away," I warned. "You'll be in more trouble than they will." When he slipped the knife back in his pocket, I left and joined Cissy. As the tallest boy raced forward brandishing a stick, the policeman stepped out from behind the chestnut wagon. He grabbed him and the other boys fled.

"Don't tell Mama how we saved the paper boy's life," Cissy said as we walked home. "She'll be worried."

But will the paper boy ever be safe? I wondered. He had only been trying to hold on to honest work.

Horatio Alger could make his stories end the way he wanted. In Gran's tales nobody was ever hurt. But the true stories were different. It would be wrong to raise Edmund's hopes about supporting his mother as a newsboy.

∞

The next day, my aunt's voice rang from the hall. "Jean, you can't leave without so much as a day's notice. I'll not give you a reference despite the fine work you've done here."

"I won't stay where I'm called Bridget, like I'm some papist."

"Well, you're the first to leave for that reason," Delia replied.

Jean Campbell continued firmly, "Maybe the Catholic girls don't mind being called Bridget no matter what their name is, and treated like they're no more than arms and legs to fetch and carry for her up there. But I've a sister in Lowell, and Boots Cotton Mill is hiring."

"Mill work is hard, Jean. Many girls lose a finger or worse, the rate they're pushed."

"The work may be hard, but here, I'm at the old lady's beck and call day and night."

"Suit yourself," my aunt said. "But I wish you would think it over."

"There's nothing to think about."

Jean's tread was firm on the back staircase. Fifteen minutes later the door to the servants' entrance slammed shut. Delia came in and sat at the kitchen table with a distracted look.

Mrs. Rafferty harrumphed from the drying room, "We can do without the likes of that one and her Belfast ways."

"I'm not so sure," Delia replied. "Jean's a smart girl. I've never had to explain a thing twice to her." She turned to me. "Picking up the photographs is out of the question today. It's Theresa's day off, and I can't leave the house short-handed."

"If we wait, the pictures won't get there for Christmas."

My aunt rose, her chin set and a scowl lining her forehead. "I'll go to Belchers myself, but first I have a few words to say upstairs."

As I listened to her firm, quick steps on the stairs, I looked anxiously over at the cook. She shook her head. "I wouldn't want to be on the receiving end of those words. It's not often your aunt gets her dander up, and she's usually in the right. Lady High-and-Mighty's not going to like what she's about to hear."

"I'd give half a day's wages to hear it myself," Mrs. Rafferty snapped a wet pillowcase in the drying room. "The old lady doesn't give a fig for anyone but herself. Thinks we're put on this earth to do her bidding. I couldn't count the times she's sent sheets back to be ironed over, and I've had to search to find a wrinkle."

When my aunt reappeared, dressed for town, she said, "Mary, if Mrs. Wooley doesn't ring, check in every half hour or so. But, if she even once calls you Bridget, tell me." She drew on her kidskin gloves and straightened her hat. "It shouldn't take more than a few hours to pick up the photographs and do a few errands."

I had not had to go to Mrs. Wooley since I'd arrived, and dreaded the sound of the bell. When half an hour passed, I listened at the bottom of the front stairs for any stirring. I would have to go up and check her.

But first I stood beneath Mrs. Wooley's portrait and resolved that I would not be afraid of her, nor let her call me Bridget. I would be polite, and do what she asked, but I would not consider myself a pair of arms and legs put on this earth to do her bidding. I glared at the handsome, haughty face looking down on me, and said under my breath, "You are no more important than anyone else in this house. The only reason we are here is because you pay us."

I tiptoed up the back staircase, and peered around her half-open door. Lying on her side, her legs drawn up, she looked smaller. She was rubbing one hand with the other, the way Gran did when her rheumatism bothered her.

A lump rose in my throat, recalling the words I had addressed to the picture, as well as the words Mrs. Rafferty and Jean Cameron spoke. It was true. The only reason we were at Sabine Street was that she paid us. But maybe she felt no one gave a fig about her, either.

I tiptoed back down the stairs. Marie and Cissy were resting on the top floor as they did every day for an hour or so. "If the old lady's asleep," Mrs. Rafferty said as she pulled on her shabby coat, "you may as well wait 'til she rings for you. No use stirring up trouble for yourself."

As soon as the laundress was gone, I placed a small potato into the oven beside the baking bread. Half an hour later I wrapped it in a linen napkin and went back upstairs. Edith Wooley was on her back, her mouth slightly open, her right hand lying in the palm of the left. Carefully, so as not to wake her, I slipped the potato into her hand the way I'd seen Gran do, when the ache in her knuckles could only be eased by moist heat coming through a wrapped potato straight from the hearth.

Half an hour later, I looked in to check. Edith Wooley was sitting up, peering through a strange looking pair of eyeglasses on a stick. "How did this potato get in my hand?" she demanded.

"It's a cure for rheumatism," I explained. "Holding a hot potato helps my gran when her fingers get sore."

She turned it over as if she'd never seen a potato before. "Is this an Irish superstition?"

"It's not a superstition," I replied. "The heat takes away the stiffness."

"Is there nothing you Irish don't rely on the potato for?" she asked over the top of her strange glasses. I wasn't sure how she meant the remark, but I saw a flicker of a smile on her thin lips as she moved her fingers back and forth. "It seems to be helping."

I backed toward the door. "If you need another, I'll have one ready in the oven."

I was already in the hall when she called, "Thank you, Bridget."

"It's Mary, Mary Cleary," I said coming back to the door sill. "I'm Delia Reardon's niece. And it's my gran, Nora Reardon, who says it helps if you start early before the pain settles in." I didn't wait for her reply.

The oven was off, so I put a second potato on a tin plate on top of the coals in the small drying room stove because Mrs. Wooley had almost smiled, even said "thank you" rather than mumble an acceptance.

I was wrapping the second potato in a napkin when Delia came in to hang her wet coat in

the drying room. She glanced at my hand quizzically.

"I'm doing what Gran does for rheumatism," I explained. "Mrs. Wooley said it helped."

"A potato helped her?"

"You know how Gran holds a hot potato when her rheumatism bothers her." As Delia shook her head, I realized that of course she didn't know. She had never seen her mother old.

Seeing the envelope in her hand, I asked if the photographs came out well.

She shrugged. "You look very nice. I look my age."

∞

That night we went over the pictures. "You choose," Delia said.

I settled on the one where I was sitting my straightest, my hands folded in my lap, with Delia behind me, not staring ahead, but looking down at me with a soft expression. "If I have enough money left, can I buy two?" I asked hesitantly, suspecting it would take every cent I had, unless I used the money I'd hidden in the back of a drawer. And how would I explain having that money?

"I'll order both," Delia said. "Photographs are more expensive than I expected, so

this will be a Christmas present from me to you."

As our eyes met over the photographs laid in a row on the

marble-topped table, Delia sighed. "I look exactly like my mother the last I saw her. She'll be surprised. We are not alike in any other way."

I didn't answer because I suspected they were alike in one way, sharing the long unforgiving memories that Father Sheehy had warned were an Irish trait, and deserving of at least one Mass a month from him. A few old women had clutched their beads, nodding. Most of the men had squirmed in their seats, then stood in little clutches after the services, ready to debate the point with each other.

Delia was reading. I was pretending to. I had been in Boston since late summer, it was now December, and I still didn't know why Gran and Delia had quarreled. How was I ever to make peace between them?

I could only hope the pictures were a start, and that I'd find the answer soon.

CHAPTER 25

Because his mother refused to go to Chestnut Hill for Christmas, George Wooley had a large tree, several wreaths, and yards of evergreen garlands delivered to Sabine Street. As I wound sweet smelling garlands around the stair rails I worded a letter to my grandmother in my mind describing my first American Christmas.

Mrs. Wooley also refused to wear regular spectacles, and couldn't manage to turn pages with a lorgnette in one hand and a potato in the other, so I was now reading the newspaper to her. That afternoon, the old lady seemed asleep so I put the *Transcript* aside and read *Phil the Fiddler* aloud as if I were reading the obituaries and boring social events of Boston during the holiday season. After two chapters, I felt it was safe to read to myself. She immediately opened her eyes. "I don't believe anything so far-fetched could go on in this country."

I held up the book and showed her the introduction. "Horatio Alger says right here that boys do play fiddles on the streets of New York, and have to turn over every cent to the men who bought them from their parents in Italy. The families never learn that their sons work all day and are punished if they don't come back and turn in enough money."

"It couldn't possibly happen in Boston," she insisted, rearranging her pillows. "But go on with the story."

When I was hoarse, Mrs. Wooley rang for tea and two cups. As I soothed my voice with the hot liquid, the old lady said, "Such ignorance, that parents could allow a thing like that to happen?"

"They were poor and hoped their children were going on to a better life in the new world. They didn't know there were men like that, any more than you did."

She looked at me sharply. My face turned red. I had as good as called her ignorant. I took another sip of tea, trying to think of something to say.

"Eat one of the tea cakes, then read some more," Mrs. Wooley said, laying her head back on the pillow.

From then on each afternoon I carried up a tray with tea, whatever cake or biscuits Marie had on hand, and two hot potatoes wrapped in a linen napkin. As I drew near the end of *Ragged Dick*, Delia offered to buy more Alger books out of the household money, saying, "They seem to be improving her disposition, though they're not the sort of reading I'd have thought would interest her."

"The stories make the poor boys real to her, the way Gran's stories made The Tiny Tunneys and the Wee Feeneys almost real." When Delia didn't seem to know what I was referring to, I added, "Maybe she told you different stories at the story stone."

"The story stone?"

"That big rock half way to town where we'd sit and rest. You must remember how good Gran is at making up stories."

Delia shook her head. "We never stopped on the way to town, but how good my mother is at making up a story, I know all too well."

She left the room before I could ask what she meant.

∞

By Christmas Eve, the tree was trimmed and swags of holly garlanded the mantels. Thick wreaths hung on the front windows and door. My aunt tried to get Edith Wooley to come down and see how the tree looked. "'Tomorrow, perhaps,' was all she'd say." My aunt shook her head. "It's her choice."

Since it was the evening before a feast day and we wouldn't be eating meat, Marie made oyster stew for us and cooked a lamb chop for Mrs. Wooley. After dinner we sat around the trimmed tree and exchanged small presents pretending we didn't know what was inside. Marie's fruitcakes smelled of Irish whiskey. Cissy's dried orange pomanders smelled of cloves. Delia's envelopes held money. Following Marie's instructions, I had made fudge and packed it in little empty tea boxes. Theresa claimed the stores were closed when she'd gone to buy us gifts. Although she had sent a box back to her family in Ireland, I hadn't really expected her to give us presents.

Marie sniffed one of the small wrapped blocks Mrs. Rafferty had left on the kitchen table for each of us. "She's added a hint of lavender this year."

"It's soap," I guessed

"She melts down slivers of fine French soap the girls save for her wherever she's working. She always has a bar for every one in the house."

I looked away toward the trimmed tree. Not for everyone in the house. Not one of us had thought of Edith Wooley, alone by her own choice, as we made ourselves at home amid her swags and garlands. Talking and laughing in the parlor, as if we owned the place.

There was fudge left over in the pan it had cooled in. I found an extra tea box, wrapped it in tissue and tied it with a bit of ribbon from the kitchen drawer and carried it upstairs...

Edith Wooley was holding her lorgnette in one hand, a magazine in the other.

"Merry Christmas," I said laying the box on the table next to her. "It's the first fudge I ever made, but I think it came out very well. I hope you like it."

She put the magazine aside. "Why, thank you." As I left, she called after me, "Thank you, Mary. I'm sure it's delicious."

At midnight I placed a candle in the window, just as I had promised Gran. I had expected to have tears in my eyes, as I pictured my grandmother standing in the cottage window in Ballydare. But I was happy.

Now Gran had a photograph of Delia. Soon I'd have Delia and her mother at peace. I had cheered Mrs. Wooley with a bit of fudge, inspired Delia with my praise of Tom Kerrigan so he and Theresa were reunited. I would convince Delia to open a hat shop someday. Anything was possible. As I watched the swirling flakes of snow melting into the halo of the gas lamp, thinking

Mrs.Moriarty was so right. Bringing people together was a wonderful vocation.

I had no idea how quickly things were about to fall apart.

CHAPTER 26

Christmas morning, I heard my aunt say, "Dr. Dudley says you're doing yourself no good staying in bed. Pneumonia is likely to set in." She finally succeeded in getting the old lady into a becoming lavender dress and to sit in the chair by her bedroom window.

An hour later, laden with beautifully wrapped presents, her son stomped up the stairs calling out with a false sounding cheeriness, "We've come to wish you a Merry Christmas, Mother. You should come out and see the countryside with the snow on the trees." I didn't hear her reply but doubted she would go with them. Theresa brought a pot of hot chocolate and matching flowered cups and saucers up to the bedroom.

In fifteen minutes Ellen came down with her little brother by the hand. "Andrew's getting fidgety, and I was afraid he'd break something."

Cissy swooped the little boy into her arms. "Let me walk him around the house and see if he remembers where things are."

As she carried him off, Mrs. Trotter said to Ellen, "Cissy misses having you and your brother around."

"And we miss Cissy and you. My mother says our new cook is hopeless." Ellen turned to me. "Grandmother says you've been reading to her."

"We've been arguing over Phil the Fiddler. She couldn't believe people actually sold their sons to such wicked men."

Ellen's mouth fell open. "You argued with my grandmother!"

"Not in a disagreeable way. But we often hold very different opinions. When we finished she said something should be done about the situation."

Ellen shook her head. "I can't wait to tell my mother. *No one* argues with Grandmother, but are her eyes so bad she can't read?"

"No, but I think she finds it hard to turn pages with a potato in one hand and a lorgnette in the other." Recognizing how odd that sounded, I added quickly, "Holding a hot potato is an old remedy for rheumatism." I was saved from having to explain further when Theresa told Ellen her father wanted her upstairs.

The family stayed for another hour. As they were leaving, Ellen's father called us into the parlor and handed out envelopes containing a dollar for each year we had spent at Sabine Street. I was surprised to see that though I'd been there only since the summer my envelope also held a dollar.

"He's generous, like his father," Delia said as their sleigh bells faded into the distance.

"I don't deny that," Mrs. Trottier agreed. "But there's not many stayed on as we have."

A few days after New Year's we took the tree down because the needles were shedding. I hated to see it go, along with the fragrant boughs and garlands. As I unfurled the swags from the railing, I wished Theresa were there to help. She had been to a party with Tom on New Year's Eve and had come to breakfast red-eyed the next morning. Marie asked if she had a cold, but she'd said she felt fine. Marie insisted she sit with her feet in a washtub filled with hot mustard water, "just in case."

This morning Theresa hadn't come down for breakfast. Maybe she really was sick.

After I unwound the holly to the top of the front hall, I went up to her room and tapped at the door. When she didn't answer, I peeked in and saw that her bed was made. I fully opened the door. Seeing her uniform draped over the back of the chair, I entered the room. There was nothing in her dresser drawers. Mystified, I sat on the edge of her bed.

Theresa's room was bare as the day we arrived, as if she'd never been there.

CHAPTER 27

"Theresa wouldn't leave without a word," my aunt protested when I told her Theresa was missing.

"That Tom Kerrigan has turned her head, and she's run off with him. He was far too good-looking to be trusted," Mrs. Rafferty said. "I always say you have to watch out for-"

"Oh shush, Peggy," Marie snapped. "She'd not run off and marry without a priest. Theresa's never even been late for Mass."

"I'm not talking about marrying."

As the words sunk in, Cissy burst into tears and disappeared into the pantry. Mrs. Trottier whacked the dough as if it were an enemy. Delia, for once, slumped in her chair.

I turned and fled to my room. I sat on the edge of my own bed, shivering as I recalled Aggie's warning. "There's many a man would take advantage of a young girl's innocence." What awful fate might Theresa face if she had her innocence taken advantage of?

Delia put off telling Mrs. Wooley that Theresa was gone, until we checked the silver.

"I knew she wouldn't steal it," I said as we returned the serving forks to their green bags. But as soon as I could, I ran up to the nursery, and searched in every corner, opened drawers, and looked under the bed. The little monkey with the key in the back was gone.

As the light faded, I read to Mrs. Wooley with the proper inflection, but in the back of my mind I was wondering if Theresa had packed the toy monkey in the Christmas box that she'd sent to Ireland.

The next morning, as Mrs. Rafferty exchanged a cooling iron for one that was steaming, she launched into a tirade. "From the moment I set eyes on Tom Kerrigan I was suspicious. You can't trust a man who could charm the birds from the trees, I always say. He can twist a young girl around his little finger with his flattery-"

Mrs. Trottier cut her off. "And is it personal experience you're speaking from, Peggy Rafferty?" The laundress went back to ironing and didn't speak for the rest of the day.

My aunt decided to look for a living-out girl who could fill in for Theresa. "She may regret leaving and come back," she said, sounding as if she didn't really believe her own words. "She could have complained to Tom about how cranky Mrs. Wooley can be, and he told her of some place better."

"Would you take her back?" I asked in surprise.

"Only if she had a good enough explanation."

But what could be a good enough explanation, I wondered as I compared the English and Latin versions of the prayers in my missal, trying to relate them to the lessons in a first year Latin book. Delia was hemming a skirt, sewing three tiny stitches where Aunt Aggie would have been satisfied with one. A line deep furrowed her brow. I knew she not only felt responsible for Theresa, she liked her. She'd given her advice on where to shop. How much to pay for things. Arranged her hours so she could go out with Tom evenings and even an occasional afternoon. There weren't many servants given that much freedom. It was hard to imagine what Theresa's explanation for leaving would be.

A living-out girl arrived the next morning. Bridget Mahoney was a neighbor of Mrs. Rafferty who could work three days a week, as that was the only time her sister was free to take care of her baby. Bridget was short, stout, and covered with freckles, and accomplished more than most girls would in twice the time. By the end of the week she was flying through the rooms with a new Bissell Carpet Sweeper she'd encouraged my aunt to buy. She gulped down her noon meal, ignoring Cissy who tried to talk with her. We neither liked nor disliked her, and I'm sure she felt the same way about us. I was beginning to miss Theresa's chatter, even about Tom, although I was now seeing Tom Kerrigan more and more through Mrs. Rafferty's eyes.

On Saturday evening, the usual time Tom came for Theresa, there was a knock on the door to the servants' entrance. Delia answered it." "So, it's you." she snapped. "What have you to say, showing up as brazen as can be?"

"Brazen? Aren't I using the servants' entrance as I always do? I've come to take Theresa out." Tom Kerrigan followed Delia into the kitchen, his hat in his hand. "If she's not free tonight, I'll understand."

My aunt faced him squarely. "Theresa Noonan has not been seen since right after New Year's."

"Theresa's not been seen?" Tom grabbed the back of a chair and steadied himself. "I brought her back safe and sound after a party at Dan O'Connell's."

"What did you do to make her run off?" my aunt asked icily.

He turned red with either anger or embarrassment. "I've done nothing forward-or improper. I brought her safely to the door and asked her to marry me as soon as I'd saved a few more dollars." Then his face paled. "Something-or-someone-"

As Cissy clapped her hands to her mouth, I saw that she had bitten her nails to the quick. Her mother put an arm around her. "What is it, Cissy? If you know something, don't be afraid to tell us. It's for Theresa's own good."

"I can't tell, Mama. It would be a sin."

"Cissy, we'll not get a moment's peace till we know where Theresa went."

Cissy placed her hand on her heart. "I swore and hoped to die, that-" She floundered as if she were trying to remember exactly what she had promised. "Theresa said I wasn't to let one word pass my lips. Not one single word."

"Wouldn't you rather tell us than the police?" Delia asked impatiently.

"Don't badger her, Delia," Marie protested. "You can see what a state she's in."

∞

I took Theresa's place drying the dishes that night. Though I tried to get Cissy to talk, she sniffled and wiped her eyes with the edge of her apron, and didn't say a single word.

Tom returned the next morning, and again in the afternoon. By the end of the week there were circles under his eyes. He pleaded and cajoled," Tell us, Cissy. You know where Theresa has gone, don't you?"

"I can't talk about it," she said, her jaw set firmly. "She made me swear, and it would be a sin to tell."

As we ate on Friday night, I tried a different approach. "Poor Tom's probably searching through alleys this very night, trying to find if Theresa's freezing to death in the cold. Or maybe she's begging scraps of food from strangers." As Cissy's lower lip trembled, I gave an exaggerated sigh. "You and Theresa used to light candles that she'd find Tom, and now he's the one sick with worry that she's shivering and hungry with her little bit of money running out."

"She's not shivering or hungry," Cissy muttered through clenched teeth..

Marie started to speak, but Delia put her fingers to her lips. I continued evenly, "Tom will be glad about that, even if he doesn't know where she is." I waited, hoping she'd say more, then decided not to push further. However, as I cut into a slice of apple pie, I sighed. "Theresa would have loved this. But at least we know she isn't starving. I hope she's not working in a pub where there's a lot of brawling and drinking. Tom could get hurt when he goes in to rescue her."

Cissy stopped chewing her nails. "Theresa's not in a pub. She's making boots. "

"Boots!" her mother exclaimed. "Is it the shoe factories in Brockton, or Fall River she's gone to?"

"Boots is all I can say. I can't tell you where," Cissy insisted.

Delia walked over and laid her hand on Cissy's shoulder. "As long as we know she's safe, you don't have to say another thing."

Looking relieved, Cissy finished her dessert. When she was running water in the pantry sink, my aunt whispered, "It must be Boots Cotton Mill in Lowell. Jean Campbell said they were hiring."

"We'll tell Tom in the morning," Marie whispered back.

"No. Not yet. I'd like to hear what Theresa has to say, first. We've only heard Tom's side of the story." Delia turned to me. "You handled Cissy very adroitly, Mary. We'll take the train to Lowell tomorrow and maybe you'll do as well talking with Theresa."

As soon as I finished drying the dishes, I hurried upstairs and opened the dictionary. As I ran my fingers along words beginning with A and D, my aunt said, without lifting her eyes from her book, "It's spelled a-d-r-o-i-t-l-y, Mary."

CHAPTER 28

I had watched trains pull out of Galway, so I was prepared for noise and smoke, but not for the sudden lurching as we started out of North Station. Straightening myself as the conductor took our tickets, I smiled, hoping to look as if I'd taken trains all my life.

We passed shabby tenements and lines of frozen laundry swinging stiffly in the alleyways. The people on the streets reminded me of those back home. A black shawled woman could have been Mrs. Slattery hurrying to Reardon's for a packet of tea or a bit of sugar. An old man sat on his back steps smoking a long clay pipe, reminded me of Granda. Two young women walked with rosy-cheeked toddlers. The surroundings couldn't have been less like Ballydare, but the faces were the same.

When we crossed a river, the crowded alleys were replaced by run-down houses and occasional fields. Standing in dirty snow beside the tracks, two children with sooty faces, held a burlap sack between them. They grinned and waved, then ran into a field and scrambled among the weeds.

"They're picking up coal and half-burned clinkers along the tracks to take home," Delia explained. "Sometimes the engineers toss them a few pieces. It's dangerous, but they stayed back far enough."

Towns and acres of snow-covered fields seemed to repeat themselves, until the train slowed and we came into a station. The conductor called, "Lowell. End of the line.",

We stepped down into a city like no other I'd seen. Or heard. The air seemed to throb.

My aunt asked the station master for directions to the Boot Cotton Mill, and we crossed a series of canals with rushing black water. The closer we came to the long line of red brick buildings five stories high, the more the air pulsed. Steam rising from the tall chimneys showered down icy crystals, like snow falling from a clear blue sky. When we entered a wide courtyard, Delia spoke to a man pushing a cart. "Where can I speak to someone about a new employee?" Without stopping, he nodded toward a door a few hundred feet away.

A rush of steamy warm air hit us as we opened a door marked Agent's Office. The man at the desk was talking with a worker. When the thin woman left through a door into the mill the din made me cover my ears. The agent waited for my aunt to speak.

"I believe you recently hired a girl named Theresa Noonan. I'd like to find where she's living, if possible."

"If she's Irish, she's likely to be living in the Acre, but I don't keep track of their lodgings." He looked at my aunt accusingly. "If she's in any trouble she's not wanted at Boots."

"Theresa Noonan is in no trouble," my aunt replied calmly. "Mrs. George Wooley of Boston owes her a few days wages She will want to know that Theresa has received them."

All smiles, the agent rose from his chair as if he were speaking with Mrs. Wooley, herself. "Yes-yes, of course. Mr. Wooley was always asking how the girls are treated here. No finer gentleman ever lived." He looked at the clock on the wall. "In two minutes the mill hands will go home to eat. If I remember correctly, last week's new girls will come out the door next to this office." He accompanied us to the door with a smile that reminded me of the word I'd looked up a few days before.

"Wasn't he obsequious after you mentioned the Wooleys?" I asked as we waited outside.

"The Wooleys are major investors in Boots," she replied, looking amused that I'd said obsequious, a word I'd looked up in the dictionary after she'd used it the week before. A bell clanged, followed by a shudder, then a silence that could almost be felt. "They've shut down the looms." she explained

"How do people stand the noise?"

"Many lose their hearing," she said as the mill workers filed out. "Others, lose fingers in the machinery, or in time develop trouble with their lungs from the lint and the steam."

The girls hurried by, many arm-in-arm. I recognized Theresa's black coat with gray trim, and ran ahead and grabbed her sleeve. She turned in surprise, then pulled away angrily, "Cissy told! I should have known better than to tell her anything."

"She didn't really tell, Theresa. Cissy let it slip that you weren't starving and cold and had someplace to work because Tom was so worried."

Delia came toward us. "And I knew Boots was hiring. Don't blame Cissy. She won't be able to face you if you do."

"She won't be facing me. I'm not going back," Theresa said lifelessly. She was no longer the girl who'd twirled around in the kitchen showing off a new scarf or pin, as she waited for Tom.

"But why? Why, Theresa?" I pleaded. "Is it anything we've said or done?"

My aunt cut in, "It's Tom Kerrigan, isn't it? It's something he's said or done."

"Tom's done nothing. I can't be seeing him, that's all." Theresa walked away. When we caught up with her she was crying.

Delia handed her a lace-edged handkerchief. "If Tom's done nothing wrong, you can't run off without an explanation. Maybe there's been some misunderstanding between you."

"It's not a misunderstanding. It's something I can't put off facing any longer." Theresa's face crumpled. She sobbed, "I won't marry a drunkard with a drink in his hand from one end of the night to the other. Always the life of the party, with the singing and the stories. I won't be living the same life my mother does."

"Then you must tell Tom that," Delia said firmly. "Face him directly. He may be willing to change."

She shook her head emphatically. "I can't take the chance. I'll believe him the first time he promises, then he'll be promising again and again. If I come back to Boston, if we even talk about it, I know I'll marry him."

My aunt put her hand on Theresa's arm. "Come back and at least get this out in the open." Then she spoke softly, but I heard every word. "You won't find anyone like Tom Kerrigan, again,

Theresa. You'll be comparing every man you meet to him, and they'll all be found wanting." Her voice choked, and I felt like crying myself .

Now I was sure. Delia *had* loved someone as much as Theresa loved Tom. Had Gran been the cause of her losing him? Done something so terrible that Delia hadn't spoken to her in years?

Theresa dabbed at her cheeks and handed the kerchief back. "I've got to go, or I'll miss my meal. And don't be telling Tom Kerrigan where I am. I don't want to see him again."

She walked off, head down, hunched against the wind, her black coat with its gray trim and fur collar completely out of place at Boots Cotton Mill.

"What will we tell Tom?" I asked my aunt, as Theresa disappeared into the crowd.

"The truth," Delia said emphatically "Nothing more. Nothing less."

CHAPTER 29

The next evening Tom Kerrigan stammered, "Why? Why would Theresa think I'm a drunkard?"

"She says you've always a drink in your hand. It's that and the singing and being the life of the party."

Delia gestured toward a chair. Tom remained standing. "Holding onto a drink is a trick I learned from Dan O'Connell, so no one will press another on me Dan went to so many meetings where the whiskey flowed, his wife made him take the pledge." He removed his overcoat, and after Marie checked the pot roast and tactfully left the room, he took the chair opposite my aunt.
"As for the singing and being the life of the party, it's not bothered Theresa before. Why should she suddenly-?"

"Because you asked her to marry you. She's afraid to marry a man who drinks too much." Delia called over to me. "Tell Tom what you told me last night, Mary."

Reluctantly, I sat down. I described the Folly Road, too far out for barefoot children to walk to school in winter. The single boiled potato the Noonan boys carried for lunch, often without even a pinch of salt. Finally, Tim Noonan, going from door to door, begging for a few cents for drink.

When I finished, Tom rose from the straight back chair. "Theresa should know me better. She knows I'm saving money. Dan O'Connell says once I'm a citizen, I'll rise far in politics. He brushed a lock of hair from his forehead. "She should have told me the glass bothered her."

"And you should have told her why you were carrying it." Delia stood up. "If her father promised to stop drinking many times, it won't be easy to convince her that you haven't been filling that glass throughout the evening."

"Theresa's father never promised to take the pledge, Tom." I suggested hesitantly. "If you take the pledge, that'll make her believe."

For the first time since he'd learned about Theresa's disappearance, Tom laughed. "Take the pledge, and me not even liking the taste of whiskey. But I'll do it, as long as she understands I've no drinking problem." He drew a large watch from his pocket. "I'll catch the next train to Lowell." As Cissy peeked around the pantry door, he called to her with a smile, "Thank you, Cissy, for letting us know where Theresa is."

Cissy crossed the threshold, wringing her hands. "Oh, but I didn't tell where she was. You can ask Miss Reardon. You must make Theresa believe that."

"Don't you worry. I'll convince her," Tom said, shrugging into his overcoat.

After the door to the servants' entrance clicked shut, my aunt said, "It's convincing Theresa he won't keep drinking that's going to be hard."

CHAPTER 30

Tom Kerrigan took the pledge and immediately caught a train to Lowell. Theresa returned with him, and we were treated once again to her constant chatter about how wonderful Tom was. How after a year, when he had actually proved that he would not take a drink, they were to be to be married. Then his great future in politics! And the grand house they would surely have someday, with indoor plumbing like Sabine Street. We were all happy for her, particularly Cissy, who listened and smiled as if she were getting married herself.

At Mrs. Wooley's request, I was now answering her bell in the afternoon. At the first ring, I slipped two hot potatoes into my apron pocket and went upstairs. Mrs. Wooley was propped up in bed. "Ellen brought this book to me yesterday," she said, wriggling around for a more comfortable position. "I question what her parents allow her to read. No respectable merchant in Boston sells *The Adventures of Tom Sawyer*. It's a disgraceful example of disobedience in children. We'll begin it and see." She settled back against the pillows, her face set in judgment.

I read until the light was fading and my throat dry. When I coughed, she told me to put the book aside and ring for tea. She lay with her eyes closed for a few minutes, then said, "Billy Banks. That was his name. Now, he could have tricked another boy into whitewashing a fence."

"My cousin Jamesy could, too," I said. "Was Billy Banks your cousin?"

"No. Billy was a farm boy I haven't thought about in years." The edge to her voice was gone.

"The winter I turned eight there was an outbreak of smallpox. When a black wreath appeared on our street, my parents sent me to the Banks' farm in Concord where one of the servant girls had come from. Mrs. Banks insisted I go outside everyday. 'Get some roses in your cheeks,' she'd say."

"You must have loved being on a farm."

She shuddered. "I hated it at first. I was terrified of the cows and pigs, and stayed far away from the barns. One afternoon a swarm of children raced across the field jeering, "City Girl, City Girl, thinks she's such a pretty girl," because I was carrying a fur muff instead of wearing mittens. They knocked me down and rubbed my cheeks with snow." Her wrinkled hands went to her face as if she could still feel the sting.

"Was Billy Banks one of them?"

"No, and when he heard what they'd done, he promised they would never hurt me again." She gave a slight chuckle, adding, "When his mother said 'What rosy cheeks you have today, Edith,' he winked. I knew I wasn't to tell what happened. By the next afternoon, Billy had piled up a huge mound of snow in the field where they'd rubbed snow on me. He'd dipped at least a hundred snow balls in water the night before, so they were frozen hard. When the ruffians trooped out from the line of trees that separated the farms, there was whooping and hollering on all sides as we hurled ice balls at those wretched children." She paused, her eyes crinkling. "My mother and father would have been horrified."

She lay back and was still for a few moments and then said in a lower voice, "No gift has thrilled me as much as those snowballs. I followed Billy Banks after that as if he were the prince in all the fairy tales."

"Did you and Billy remain friends?"

"No, I never saw any of the Banks after the smallpox scare."

That evening, as I turned up the wicks on the lamps, I looked up at the painting of Mrs. Wooley. I could never have pictured that proud lady in her rings and necklace as a frightened child if she hadn't told me about Billy Banks.

She had told Ellen over and over about every piece of jewelry she had been given. Too bad she hadn't told her about the thrilling gift of snowballs.

CHAPTER 31

"It looks like a present," Theresa said the next day, as she handed me a heavily wrapped package with a smile.

I tore away the wrapping. The months and miles across the Atlantic disappeared as if I'd never left Ballydare.

The photographer who came through the village about once a year had caught the bottom edge of the sign, Reardon's Store. Aunt Aggie held one twin. Uncle Pat the other. Jamesy and Maggie stood beside Gran's rocker, holding up their bags of marbles. I brushed aside a twinge of jealousy seeing Lizzie looking up at Gran instead of at the camera.

I shuffled through the separate letters, and read Gran's first.

Dear Mary,
Just a note, to let you know that I am well and very busy.
Vincent is a colicky baby, as you were. But the colic will pass
in a few months I am sure. Meanwhile, it is good to know that
I am a help to Aggie.
I am so proud of you. To think you are studying Latin and
French and reading all those great books that will teach you
about the world. You have no idea how much joy your letters
bring.

Love,
Gran

Then Jamesy's. "Thank you for the marbles. I have won all

Maggie's marbles twice." Followed by Maggie's. "Thank you for the lovely red, white, and blue marbles. Especially for the big one. It is my lucky marble and I won back all my marbles twice with it."

Uncle Pat thanked me for the pipe tobacco, said there was grumbling throughout the land because once again families were being evicted. The Healey's cottage had been burned to the ground only a few days ago. He hoped there wouldn't be an uprising.

Aggie's bold handwriting was on three letters. One for me. One for Cissy. The third, addressed to Delia Reardon, was sealed with a single drop of candle wax. I brought it straight to my aunt. "There's a letter for you, from Ireland," I said, watching her face.

She looked up from a column of figures. "Just put it on the desk, Mary. I'm in the middle of adding." Stunned that she could wait to read the only letter she'd received from her family, I left without mentioning the picture.

If Delia was indifferent to the family in Ireland, Cissy was not. "They're wrapped in the blankets I made," she exclaimed. "Which one is Vincent? Which one is Francis?"

I turned the photograph. "It says Aunt Aggie's holding Vincent. Uncle Pat has Francis"

She peered into the tiny faces "They're beautiful and so big. I'll have to make them bigger blankets."

I hadn't noticed that Aggie had wrapped Cissy's blankets over heavier, warmer ones. When Cissy went upstairs with her letter, Marie looked at the photograph. "A lovely family," she said with a smile as she handed it back. "I'm glad you and Theresa tell Cissy about the little ones back home. She thinks of them almost as her own family."

Throughout dinner Cissy chatted about the colors she would choose for the next blankets. Marie commented on the family resemblances in the picture. Still, my aunt didn't ask to see the photograph.

When we were upstairs, I thrust it between her newspaper and eyeglasses. "That's Aggie and Vincent," I said. "Aggie thanked Cissy for the blankets, even wrapped the baby in one so she could see. This picture must be a thank you for the ones you sent."

"Those pictures were from *you*, Mary."

Delia looked down at the figures, in everyday clothes, unlike in the photographs taken on Tremont Street. I waited, hoping she would break down and cry, admitting how much she missed her family. Instead she handed me the picture, saying, "Aggie has a good face. I'm glad my brother married a nice woman. He deserved one." She went back to reading *The Pilot*. I placed the picture on the table, facing her so she'd have to look at it.

After we'd read for an hour she said, "It's time to go to bed, Mary." As I started out the door she called, "Don't forget your picture."

"I'm leaving it in here where the light is better."

My aunt put her paper down. "I know what you're trying to do, Mary. I will write to Aggie and tell her I am happy for her and Pat and that they have a lovely family. But everything I have to say to my mother has already been said. I don't want you in the middle of it. You love her and she loves you, and that's the way it should be."

I jumped at the chance to get things out in the open. "But maybe it's just a misunderstanding between you and Gran. Like between Theresa and Tom. Once they talked things over-"

Delia peered over the rim of her glasses, her face as set as a statue, her voice as cold. "My mother knew exactly what she was doing, and I will never forgive her."

Before I undressed, I propped the photograph against a little vase on my dresser. In the dim glow of candlelight, Gran's stern expression looked as unforgiving as Delia's. Though for weeks I hadn't thought of Mrs. Moriarty, I wished I could ask her, *"Was there ever a time when, no matter how you tried, you couldn't keep your family in touch?"*

A week later, Theresa handed me a second letter from Ireland. Knowing my reply couldn't have arrived back so soon, I tore it open anxiously.

On a single sheet my grandmother told me that Edmund Burke's mother had died. She'd been wandering and a freezing rain had driven her into an abandoned cottage. By the time they found her, pneumonia had set in. She thought I should know before I wrote to Edmund again.

I stared at the sheet of paper. How could I write to Edmund? What could I say? For the rest of the day I rejected lines. "I am sorry to hear…I was sorry to hear…I am sorry to learn…I am sorry to know." Nothing sounded right. There just weren't any words that would do. I read to Mrs. Wooley an extra half hour, lingered over Latin declensions, even reread a story in a *Saint Nicholas Magazine*, rather than face writing to Edmund.

I didn't mention the letter to Delia. If she had no interest in her own family, why should she hear any news from Ireland? I didn't tell her the candle I lit after Mass was for Poor Mae Burke, who would forever be that to me, now. I said a decade of the rosary for the repose of her soul each night, feeling guilty because I'd once prayed that Edmund be able to keep going to school. I hadn't meant that his mother would die. For close to two weeks I promised myself, "Tomorrow I will write. Tomorrow I will write."

But it was Edmund who wrote first. I was setting the chimney into a parlor lamp when Delia handed his letter to me.

> *Dear Mary,*
>
> *Your Grandmother told me she wrote to you when my mother died. I am glad she did, because it makes it easier for me to write this letter. I'm sure you found it hard to write to me, not knowing what to say and all.*
>
> *But I have to let you know I'll soon be leaving Ballydare. Johnnie Boyle's brother says they're hiring in Liverpool, and that there's almost as many Irish there as English. Father Sheehy doesn't want me to go. He's trying to get me to enter the minor seminary in Galway. He says I wouldn't be obligated to take final vows to be a priest. But I know they would try to persuade me. I promised him I'd wait until after turf cutting in May.*
>
> *Yesterday, I walked up to Ashmont to think about it and looked down at the story stone. Remember the happy times we sat there listening to your grandmother? Of course, this time of year it was bleak, no green at all, just miles of stones and chimneys telling their own sad stories of Ireland.*
>
> *When I saw the Healey's chimney sticking out, still black with soot. I don't know what came over me, Mary. I started hurling rocks downhill, angry as the old men grumbling*

about driving the English out, the ones drinking their lives away at the unfairness of it all. I knew how they felt. And that it was a sorry sort of priest I'd be with so much bitterness choked up inside of me.

I tried to explain it to Father Sheehy. He said recognizing those feelings in myself would make me a better priest, help me to understand others. But I know I've not the vocation. It would be wrong to take a place from a boy who has.

Meanwhile, people are being generous. Tomorrow, I'll be hacking away at the weeds in the Dinsmore's garden. I do the odd job for your uncle Pat. When we have a patch of good weather, he'll teach me how to fix the thatch on your grandmother's cottage. I'll stay out there while I'm working on it.

But my mind is made up. I have to leave Ireland. I'll be in Liverpool before summer is through. Until then, you can write to me here, and I hope you do.

Your friend,
Edmund Burke

"I should have written first," I said over and over as Delia led me into the parlor and made me sit down on the rosewood chair.

"Do you mind?" she asked, taking the letter from my hand. She sat opposite me in the lady's chair and as she read, tears rolled down my cheeks. All I'd needed to write was I'm sorry your mother died. It wouldn't have mattered what words I used. I was trying to stifle the tears when Delia asked, "How old is Edmund?"

"He'll be fourteen in March," I replied sniffling.

"He's a very bright boy." She looked at the letter again. "Good in school work?"

"Even missing a lot, he stayed ahead of everyone else his age."

As my aunt re-read the letter, I remembered the many days Edmund hadn't come to school and everyone knew he was searching for his mother. There were several times when half of Ballydare went exploring hollows, bushes, and ruins of abandoned or burned out houses.

Now Edmund was going off to work in a factory;. to England,

the country he blamed for so much of the misery of the famine years.

My aunt and I sat quietly in the richly furnished parlor, the only sound the ticking of the hall clock, then the chimes at the half hour.

I had no idea at that time what was going on in Delia's mind.

CHAPTER 32

My aunt hadn't handed Edmund's letter back. After three days, I looked for it on her bureau. Sorting through opened envelopes, I peeked into the thickest to see if his letter had been slipped inside. Folded around a stack of money, a sheet marked, Emerald Row 22, 24, 26, 28 ended with a scrawled note and a flourished signature.

Reilly--#26-- Three months in arrears.
I will take care of this immediately. J.J Mc Guire.

I remembered Mrs. Moriarity's warning to Ned Kelley. "Stay away from Emerald Row and Ann Street with their taverns and fighting. There are no worse streets in all of Boston."

Much as I didn't want to believe it, it was clear that my proper aunt, who never left the house without gloves, or was late for Mass, owned 22,24,26,and 28 Emerald Row. But surely her property would be in good repair, and her tenants respectable. Nevertheless, I wanted someday to see Emerald Row for myself.

That night Delia handed me Edmund's letter. "I've had a Mass said for Edmund's mother. It'll be on a weekday so we won't be able to attend, but a dozen old ladies never miss daily Mass. Mae Burke will be well prayed for."

I thanked her, put Emerald Row out of my mind, and turned my thoughts to a more immediate and difficult task. What could I say, how could I write a letter to Edmund?

∞

A few days later we woke up to a foot of snow. The S.S. Pierce man made a morning delivery in a wagon on runners called a pung. At noon Ellen appeared at the front door, red-faced and laughing. A sleigh and driver waited at the curb.

"This has to be the last big snow of the year," she said breathlessly to my aunt. "My mother will be hours at the Woman's Journal and says I can keep the sleigh and go any where I want. I'd like Mary to come with me to the Athenaeum. It would be very educational."

I was washing the mirror on the hall tree, and quickly wiped my hands on my apron. Delia was encouraging any influence on me by Ellen Wooley, and would probably agree.

"Can I?" I asked. "I can go up and change."

"Yes, you may, Mary." Delia answered, slightly stressing the "may".

"I'll say 'Hello' to my grandmother while you change."

As Ellen ran up the front hall stairs, my aunt said, "The Athenaeum is a private library, so wear your new blue dress, "

In my wool dress and wool coat, I was almost too warm under the carriage robes. Snow swirled around in huge flakes and the streets were practically deserted. The Athenaeum was closed because of the weather, and many of the smaller shops had shut their doors.

"We'll go to the tea room, Dinny," Ellen called to the driver "You can pick us up in about forty minutes." As he dropped us off, she said, "He'll have time for a bowl of stew. It wouldn't be right to keep him sitting in the cold."

Ellen ordered a pot of hot chocolate and a plate of little cakes decorated with tiny silver balls, or leaves and flowers of pink and green. "Don't we look like proper ladies eating our petits fours?" she asked between bites. "Should we be discussing the shortcomings of our friends? Of course, my mother and her friends are discussing women's suffrage. Certainly nothing trivial."

"We could talk about literature," I suggested in what I considered a proper Boston accent. "Horatio Alger has an interesting view on how to get ahead in the world."

She gave an exaggerated sigh. "But sure and don't his generous benefactors always turn up at the right moment? Louisa May Alcott would have been more clever, don't you think?"

I couldn't stop laughing "You sound just like my aunt Delia."

"And you sounded *almost* like my mother."

We continued laughing and talking, I attempting a Boston accent, Ellen sounding more and more like Delia. When two middle-aged women frowned, we went outside. The snow was floating down in even larger flakes. "Is there anywhere you'd like to see while we have the sleigh, Mary?" Ellen asked. "Tomorrow, the roads will likely be slush.'

I grabbed the opportunity that might never come again. As if it were an off-handed suggestion, I said, "Well, on the ship I heard about a street called Emerald Row. I may recognize some people there."

When Dinny arrived, Ellen asked if he knew where Emerald Row was. He frowned. "You shouldn't be going to a place like that, Miss Ellen. A very rough element lives there."

"But we'll be with *you*, Dinny. You'd be a match for anyone."

He laughed. "I'll drive you to the corner, but we won't be stopping."

The sleigh moved swiftly along the nearly deserted streets. The streets became narrow and shabby. After a few turns he slowed down. Taverns stood on each corner of Emerald Row. A man bundled in an overcoat stumbled out of one, bumping into a younger man going in.

"Well, here we are, and I hope you've seen enough," Dinny called back.

I whispered to Ellen, "I'd hoped to go down it."

When she told Dinny to turn into Emerald Row, he shook his head, and shrugged. I strained to read the numbers on the run-down houses. In front of number 26, a small crowd watched a shawl-wrapped woman help a burly man on a crutch down the steps. Half a dozen children followed with bundles and odds and ends of furniture. The road was too jammed and narrow for the sleigh to turn. Dinny pulled to a stop. "Happens all the time," he said, without a trace of sympathy in his voice. "They're being thrown out. Probably couldn't come up with the rent."

Remembering the note on Delia's bureau, I covered my mouth to keep from saying it aloud, *"Evicted? In this snow?"* A dozen children surrounded the sleigh, touching the smooth black sides, shouting, "Make the bells jingle for us, Mister."

"I see someone I know." I said, taking advantage of the fact that we couldn't move, and jumped out of the carriage.

Dinny called, "Get back in here," as I raced into the crowd. I had not lied when I said I'd seen someone I knew. The scowling man at the curb had to be J.J. McGuire. The one who had written, *Reillys three months in arrears. I'll take care of this immediately..*

I elbowed through the crowd and was shocked. Peeling paint. Rags jammed into broken window panes. Two small boys lugged a stained mattress. A little girl carried a stuffed pillow case almost as large as herself. An older girl shushed a wailing baby in a laundry basket.

When the burly man's crutch slipped, a boy caught him by the sleeve. "I'm all right, Dickie," he muttered. "It's just that rotted board."

At the name Dickie, inspiration swept over me. I pulled myself tall, like Delia, like Gran. "Mr. McGuire," I called firmly, but not so loud that my voice would carry back to the sleigh. He turned with a glare. I swallowed hard. "I have a message from my aunt, Miss Delia Reardon. The Reilly's rent has been paid by a generous benefactor." I looked straight at the boy called Dickie. "Young Dick Reilly is being rewarded for his courage and honesty."

J.J. McGuire glared, but then stepped back. I could see that he recognized me.

"Miss Reardon sent me here, hoping to stop this, Mr. McGuire," I continued, my heart thumping. I'd never told such an outrageous lie in my life.

J.J. McGuire shrugged and walked off without so much as a word to the Reillys, or to me.   Both Mr. and Mrs. Reilley stood with their mouths open. Finally, Mr. Reilly said, "What the divil have you been up to, Dickie? When was you ever honest?"

Dickie shook his head in bewilderment. "I dunno, Da. I must've forgot."

Mrs. Reilly laid a hand on her son's shoulder, and turned toward her husband. "Haven't I always told you he's a good boy at heart? You're much too hard on him, Jim." She addressed the crowd. "I told you my boy never done those things you been accusin' him of."

The Reillys immediately began carrying their meager possessions inside. From the top step, Mr. Reilly called, "Young Miss, tell the landlord this hip of mine is mending. I'll be working steady soon. He needn't be worrying about the rent again."

When I returned to the sleigh the children were patting the horse, and trying to feed it snow. Dinny said to Ellen, "Don't be telling your parents I let you come here. They'd have my head for it."

"I won't say anything, Dinny," Ellen promised as the crowd thinned and the carriage was able to turn. At the corner, several men argued loudly in front of the taverns, though it was only mid-afternoon. A group of boys jeered them on. I couldn't speak because of the conflicting feelings inside me.

For the sake of the Reillys, I was glad I had come to Emerald Row, but I was ashamed Ellen had seen the wretched conditions where every voice was Irish: even the children sounded as if they'd just stepped off the boat, though most of them had probably been born here. When we reached Tremont Street, Ellen touched my hand. "You must feel terrible to see how your friends from the boat are living, Mary. I hope they get away from that awful street soon."

I didn't say anything. Though the Reillys were not my friends from the boat, the people on Emerald Row were my own people. I was ashamed of myself for being ashamed of them. I was not only ashamed but angry. My aunt rented houses with peeling paint, rotted steps, and windows stuffed with rags, and worst of all, threw tenants out into the snow.

I thanked Ellen for inviting me to go in the sleigh with her, and then bit my tongue. The angry words I would save for Delia.

CHAPTER 33

"Are you coming down with a cold, Mary?" Marie asked as we ate that night. "You've barely touched your plate, and your eyes are red."

I gave a halfhearted cough. "The snow got into my shoes." She was all for plunging my feet in hot mustard water and making me drink ginger tea, but settled for a promise that I wouldn't stay up too late.

Delia followed me up the stairs. I had not spoken to her as we ate, only nodded when she asked if we had had a good time. As I headed toward my room she said, "Come and sit awhile. I can tell something's wrong. Have you and Ellen had a falling out?"

"No," I answered crisply. My dampened-down anger flarered. As soon as I crossed her threshold I said, "How could you throw a family out into the snow?"

Delia stiffened. "Whatever are you talking about, Mary?"

"We went to Emerald Row today. Mr. Reilly was on crutches coming down the rickety steps with his family. You're as bad as the English, not caring a bit for the people you collect rent from."

"You went to Emerald Row? With Ellen Wooley!" Delia clamped her hands to her forehead. "Of all the stupid things."

For a fraction of a second I was caught off-guard, as if I were the one in the wrong. But that feeling left as fast as it had come. "Ellen doesn't know you own those houses. She thought I was looking for people I met on the ship. I made sure she couldn't hear me tell that horrid J.J. McGuire the Reilly's rent had been paid and they could go back into the house."

"You told him *what*?"

"I told him their rent had been paid. You can take it from the money I've been saving."

Delia's eyes narrowed. "How did you know the Reilleys hadn't paid their rent? Have you been snooping among my papers."

"I wasn't snooping. I was looking for Edmund's letter."

"And just happened to read mine, I suppose?" Her eyes drilled into mine. "Mary, you know nothing--nothing at all about the kind of people who live on Emerald Row. They skip out in the middle of the night, months of back rent due. Drink half their earnings away, then drift off to some other street. They're lazy and irresponsible."

"That's the way the English talk about the Irish," I snapped back. "Saying all we know is how to grow potatoes. That we're ignorant and lazy. You're every bit as bad as the English."

"Well, I had nothing to do with any eviction. Mr. McGuire sees to the rents."

"Like the rent collectors back home, so the owners don't have to look anyone in the face, or see how miserably some people live."

Delia paced, never taking her eyes off me. "Don't think you can tell me about miserable lives, young lady. When I arrived in Boston, many who'd come during the famine still lived in attics so low they couldn't stand up. In cellars half flooded with water. I put my pride in my pocket and worked at things I never thought I'd have to do. For twelve years, I wore the same coat, saving every cent to invest in property. I've put new roofs on those houses. I have the latrines emptied regularly. I expect to receive my rents on time."

"You didn't have to throw a family into the street with their baby in a laundry basket. You've a heart of stone, just like they said back home."

Delia's lips set tight. For a moment it was like looking at Gran. "So that's how I'm talked about back there, is it? A heart of stone, indeed. After what she did to me. Her lies, and conniving. My mother's the one with the heart of stone."

"Gran only tells white lies to spare someone's feelings, and it is you that has the hard heart. Everyone in Ballydare gets letters from their daughters. You never once wrote to Gran and told her how you were."

A dam of tears burst, as I remembered my grandmother gazing at the sea as if she'd lost half her family to it. "I have money enough to go home," I said through the tears. "I'm going back on the next ship."

Delia turned her back to me. "You'll not leave while the sea is rough. In June, you may do as you please. I won't keep you here."

She rearranged letters on her bureau as if I weren't in the room. I left, banging the door with more force than I'd intended. I lifted the latch, about to apologize for the rudeness, then let it go. Why should I be sorry for slamming a door, when she was so wrong about everything else?

Reaching into the far right corner of the bureau drawer, I found the kerchief that held the money I'd hidden. With my fare clenched in my hand I leaned against the windowsill watching the flakes melt into the heat of the gas lamp. Listened to the steady drip from the eaves. Across the street a dim light glowed in a top window. I wondered if the room had heat. Because of Delia, the top floor of Sabine Street had heat. And yet she'd thrown her own tenants out into the snow.

For at least an hour I worked myself up over how much better Ireland was. In Ireland, people didn't live a few hundred feet from each other and never pass two words between them. In Ireland, only the English did wicked things.

I will be happier where I belong, I told myself, casting away Girls' Latin School. Boston University. Trying to convince myself that I wouldn't miss anything about America. Or my aunt Delia.

CHAPTER 34

When crocuses followed snowdrops along the back fence, Marie predicted an early spring. Mrs. Rafferty said there'd be another freeze and the blossoms would be nipped in the bud. But despite the warm breeze and lengthening days, my spirits hung over me like a layer of winter cloud. My aunt and I were saying little more to each other than "Pass the sugar, please" or "Yes, I would like a bit more, thank you."

One morning after Delia left the house, Marie slowed her paring knife and looked at me thoughtfully. "Your aunt hasn't asked how your French is progressing lately."

I rubbed harder on a silver bud vase I was polishing. "I won't be needing to know French. I'm going back to Ireland "

The cook put her paring knife down. "But she has such plans for you, Mary."

"They're her plans, not mine. I miss Ireland and my family."

"You're homesick, that's all. I was even homesick for Quebec, though it wasn't home, the way Ireland was." The cook glanced out the kitchen window at the crocuses "A bit of fresh air will do you good. You and Cissy could walk over to the Public Garden since there's little to do here with the old lady off to Chestnut Hill for the day."

Cissy had spent the previous afternoon at the Home of the Angel Guardians and bubbled with enthusiasm, as we passed shoots of red and green poking through beds of freshly raked soil.

"I never thought I'd have so many friends, Mary," she said taking my arm. "You and Theresa, and the sisters. Sister Patrick is my favorite. I help her in the kitchen. Then comes Sister Mary Joseph. Then Sister Mary Immaculata."

I felt like a cross old lady walking by her side. For a week, I'd read to Mrs. Wooley with barely any expression in my voice. Alone, I daydreamed about arriving in Ballydare when roses tumbled along the stone walls. Then I'd see Edmund, searching those same walls in the depth of winter. If I pictured Gran and Aggie welcoming me, I immediately wondered if I'd be in the way, now that the twins were born. Would Gran consider staying at the cottage at least during the summer months? Or was she so convinced Aggie needed her that she and I would be sharing the little room behind the store?

Cissy tugged on my sleeve. "The hurdy-gurdy, Mary. Let's go see him."

We crossed over to the common where a small crowd had gathered around the man and his monkey. "I hope he's here the next time Andrew comes, " Cissy whispered. "He loves seeing the monkey. He was so happy when I found his toy monkey and let him take it home."

For the first time in weeks, my spirits lifted. Theresa hadn't stolen the monkey after all.

Children with nursemaids clapped at the end of every song and scrambled to be the first to place a penny into the little monkey's outstretched cap. When Cissy gingerly dropped a coin, then ran backwards in tiny steps, I had to laugh myself.

We circled the Frog Pond twice. Paused to admire the dome of the Capitol shining in the early afternoon sun. By the time we'd climbed the hill to Sabine Street we were tired and thirsty.

After a glass of water, chilled with chips from the block the iceman had left that morning, I decided to go up and change my clothes. The door to the front hall was open. A single letter lay on the silver tray. Recognizing the Irish stamp, I ruled out the senders as I approached. Not Gran, Aggie or Uncle Pat. Not the downward slant of Edmund. Yet, the large block like letters were familiar.

My hand froze over the envelope that was addressed to Delia. Was Father Sheehy breaking news that was too hard for Pat or Aggie to put on paper? The way Gran had written me first, making it easier for Edmund. I wanted to tear the envelope open, but remembered Delia's anger. "Snooping around my papers."

When Delia's steps came up the brick walk, I hurried up the stairs. Looking down from the landing I saw her hand freeze over the letter as mine had. She lifted it to her chest, her other gloved left hand on her cheek. Biting her lip, she tore open the envelope and dropped onto the seat of the hall tree.

I nearly tripped, racing down the steps. "It's Gran, isn't it? He's writing that Gran…" I couldn't say the word.

"No, thank heaven. It's not that. You may as well read this yourself." She handed me the letter.

Dear Delia,

It's not often a country priest receives a letter from a bishop, particularly one from a diocese as large and far away as Boston. Needless to say, I answered him immediately that Edmund would be a fine addition to any school. The lad can hardly believe there's a scholarship waiting for him, as well as a place to stay and do chores for his upkeep.

His Grace's letter is tacked next to the map in the store. A jar on the counter is filling with pennies for his passage. Your mother counts the coins on the hour, and I suspect has slipped in a few of her own. Aggie is making the first suit the lad has ever had on his back.

I know with your generous heart, Delia Reardon, you'll be offering to pay his fare yourself. But let the people of Ballydare be a part of this grand opportunity for one of their own. You've already been an answer to their prayers.

Yours in Christ,
Francis A.Sheehy

"You took Edmund's letter to the *Bishop*. All the way to the *Bishop!*" I exclaimed, my voice cracking. "That's why I couldn't find it."

She nodded. "Edmund will be attending a preparatory school for Boston College, and living nearby with Dr Keegan and his family." She stood up, looked at herself in the mirror, shook her head, and went up the front staircase.

I climbed the back stairs slowly, to be alone and think.

CHAPTER 35

That night I tapped softly on the door between our rooms. When my aunt said, "Come in, Mary." I braced myself and lifted the latch. She was waiting, with two cups and a plate with two slices of pound cake.

"I shouldn't have spoken to you the way I did, "I said, looking down at the small rug in the doorway. "I didn't know you were going to send Edmund's letter to the Bishop."

She nodded without speaking as she poured tea into the second cup. Then, after adding milk and stirring in two teaspoons of sugar, my aunt looked at me directly and as quickly looked away. "I'd not set foot in Emerald Row in five years," she explained. "It's in a rough neighborhood, so I hired an agent to collect the rents. He's charged me for repairs which I see were never made. Mr. Reilly will collect the rents from now on, and make repairs in his spare time. He seems capable, and his son will help him build new front steps."

She raised her own cup, took a sip, and then asked with a half smile, "However did you come up with the idea a mysterious benefactor paid the back rent?"

"Ellen and I had been talking about Horatio Alger. It just popped into my head."

"And you'd be the mysterious benefactor?"

"I could take it out of my wages."

"And have enough to go home?"

I turned red and reached for a slice of pound cake. My mouth was so I could dry I could hardly swallow the small piece I broke off. I coughed and took a sip of tea.

"I never should have said you were like the English landlords. And it was Mrs. Laughlin who said you had a heart of stone. Gran never spoke against you. Gran said you were fair."

"Did she, indeed?"

Although we were facing each other, my aunt's gaze went past me as if she were looking far off. I had finished almost half my cup before she spoke again. "This afternoon, when I saw the letter from Ireland, I was afraid my mother had died. That it was too late to make peace. I'll write and say I'm sorry so many years have gone by. I've come that far, at least." Her eyes returned to mine. "But there'll always be a part of me blaming her for what she did, Mary."

I drained my cup, and before my courage failed, asked, "What *did* Gran do, Aunt Delia?"

The teapot shook as Delia picked it up "I'll make more tea. This may take a while."

I knew the direct question had taken her by surprise, and I was not surprised by the length of time passing before she returned. Her face was composed, but her hand still trembled as she filled the cups. "You know Ashmont, and the Ashtons, of course."

"I know Ashmont, but the Ashtons haven't lived there for years.'

She stopped pouring. "I always thought he'd stay on."

The puzzle pieces in my mind slipped a little closer. I waited to hear who he was. Was he the reason Gran would never go near Ashmont?

Delia tossed her head as if to rid herself of something annoying. "Well, Ashmont's where it all began and ended. Thomas Ashton was the only son. He was English. And he was Protestant. When he asked me to marry him, we knew our families, indeed the whole village, would be shocked, but we didn't care."

She took a sip of tea, her hand shaking a little less. "Tom Kerrigan gave me a start when I saw him from the swan boat. They looked so much alike, though Thomas may have been a bit taller, at least that's how I remember him."

"I asked if you'd ever seen anyone as handsome and you said, 'Not in a long long time.' "

Delia laughed slightly. "You don't miss much, Mary. I suppose it set you to wondering."

"It did." I leaned forward. "Did you always call him Thomas, not Tom?"

"He was Thomas, never Tom, to me or anyone else."

"So that's when you and Gran had the big fight?"

"Not then, Mary. It would have been better if we'd had a row right off. Better if my mother had ranted and raved, told me I was losing my immortal soul, that we'd be shunned by both sides in Ireland. I could have fought back. I'd have told her Thomas promised to bring the children up Catholic. That we'd go to Canada, or the United States if need be."

She stopped a few moments before she went on. "Oh, but my mother was far too sly for that. She asked how soon we planned to be married. When I told her in six months, she only shrugged. I should have been suspicious. But I'd never known my mother to be deceitful, so I wasn't prepared for her lies."

I braced myself, unwilling to believe my grandmother capable of any great wrong.

As if she'd read my mind, Delia continued. "I didn't know what my mother was capable of. Within the week, she must have talked with the Ashtons, written to an elderly aunt in Tyrone, and set her trickery in motion. Sweet as could be, she asked if I'd mind going up to Tyrone. Her aunt had taken a fall and needed someone with her for a few days. I was so relieved that she'd put no obstacles in our way, I was more than willing. I should have known better. My mother could be kind and generous, but she was never sweet."

I started to protest, but Delia kept on as if the feelings had been bottled inside for years. "They were all in on it. They had to be. Every time I started to pack my things and come home, Aunt Annie took a spell for the worse, and I'd write to Thomas saying I'd be gone a few more days. The stay stretched on for weeks. When I returned I was told Thomas had come to his senses and left for England."

"Didn't he get your letters?"

"My father, trusted to handle all the letters that came by post, let my mother destroy them."

On the verge of tears, I asked, "How did you find out?"

"Five years later, I saw Thomas, holding a little girl's hand as she bent down to touch the waves. I almost backed away, but he saw me. 'So! You've come back from the states for a visit?' he said, with the strangest expression on his face, as if he'd seen a ghost.

"When I told him I'd never left for the states, he lifted the child and came up from the water's edge. For an hour we sat on a beached curragh exchanging stories. His parents had told him I'd realized the marriage was unwise and gone off to a cousin in America. Then they'd sent him on some contrived business to be taken care of in England."

The lines on her face deepened. "There was no cousin in America. There was no real reason for him to be in England."

"They lied!"

"Yes, Mary. His mother, and my mother, both."

Her voice grew even more bitter. " For almost five years I believed their pack of lies. Can you blame me for being angry?" Without waiting for an answer, she picked up a newspaper, rattling the pages, not stopping long enough to read anything.

Ten minutes passed before she spoke again. More calmly, she described the temper she'd flown into, the words hurled on both sides, too cutting ever to be forgotten. I listened in silence, remembering Delia's plea to Theresa outside Boots Mill. "You will never find anyone like Tom. You'll be comparing every man you meet to him and they'll all be found wanting."

I could not blame Delia for being angry, but this was a side of my grandmother I had never seen, and did not want to see. Gran had hidden the lies she'd told Delia from everyone. Uncle Pat didn't know why his sister stormed out of the house. The neighbors believed Delia Reardon had a heart of stone. Even Father Sheehy had been surprised that I didn't know my mother had a sister.

When Delia picked up "*The Boston Pilot*" I opened a book in which I had no interest, knowing the conversation was ended. The lamp sputtered and Delia looked at the clock on the dresser. "Ten-thirty, already. Time for you got to bed." She turned up the wick half an inch. "Your grandmother has been good to you all these years. Your feelings for her should not change."

I lay awake mulling over what my aunt had told me. Finally, I turned my back to the strip of light under the door between our rooms. Nothing I could say or do would undo what had happened between my aunt and my grandmother.

I woke before the first light of dawn, my sheet and flannel blanket in a tangle. I'd dreamed I was on the *Halcyon*, racing back and forth, from side to side. Struggling to catch my breath, I stopped in front of Mrs. Moriarity. "Which way are we headed?" I asked. "America? Ireland?"

Without raising her eyes from the tangle of yarn she was unraveling, Mrs. Moriarity answered, "You don't have to take sides."

CHAPTER 36

The next week Theresa turned her head from me as we passed in the back hallway. I couldn't imagine what had happened. She had been happy the day before when a letter came from her little brother saying he'd won a spelling bee. Later, because it was her afternoon off, instead of going out to shop or at least to look in the store windows, she stayed in her room.

Marie Trottier noticed the change, too. "Something's bothering Theresa", she said as she rolled out a pie crust. "I'd hate to think she's had a quarrel with Tom." She turned the crust over, gave it a light dusting of flour, then went to the pantry. She returned with a plate of cookies and put it in my hands. "She'll open the door if you tell her you have lemon snaps."

"I hope so," I replied, though I doubted it would be that easy.

I went up the back staircase wondering how I'd get Theresa to tell me what was wrong. I knocked at her door softly, no answer, and tried again. Still no answer. I put my ear to the door, and heard her crying. "Mrs. Trottier sent up some lemon snaps." I called in.

"Go away," she answered, lifelessly.

"Not until you tell me why you are crying."

"I said go away," she snapped. Then through the closed door I heard crying turn into sobs. I lifted the latch and peeked in. Theresa was facing the window, her body shaking.

"What's wrong, Theresa" I asked. "What's happened?"

She whirled around. Her cheeks were blotched with tears. She tried to speak but could only manage to stammer. "I'm... I'm..."

I waited in the doorway, stunned, recalling Aunt Aggies' warning. *The things a young girl must know after a certain age.* Josie and Mamie snickering. Aggie's voice again. *A man who takes advantage of a girl.* But surely not Tom!

Fortunately, before I could say another word, Theresa sputtered through choking sobs, "I'm, I'm ignorant, Mary. Ignorant. I can barely read and write."

As she collapsed onto her bed I crossed the room and sat beside her. "How can you say that? You write letters home. Just yesterday, you read us the letter your brother sent."

"And it was a better letter than I could write." She sniffled. "Danny's only nine. And he won a spelling bee.... a *spelling bee,* Mary. I can't even follow the newspapers." After a few more sobs she sat up and took a few deep breaths. "When I'm with Tom and all those people he's meeting, I don't know what they are talking about. I try to read the newspapers but it takes so long to sound out the big words that I forget what the beginning of the sentence means."

Remembering all the times Theresa had missed school, how she'd eventually stopped coming at all, I understood. She had told Mrs. Wooley that was neat. I had seen her signature, which was much neater than mine. But she hadn't tried to read *"Little Women"* or any book I'd suggested before I stopped making suggestions.

I sat by her side for a few minutes trying to think of comforting words, then settled on the only answer that had any meaning.

"I'll be right back," I said. I crossed the narrow hall to my room and sorted through the books Ellen left behind. Within two minutes I found Phil the Fiddler. It was short, simply written, and the sad story would make her think of her brothers, especially Danny, and keep turning the pages.

I returned to her room and held up the thin book. "This is about a poor Italian boy sold by unsuspecting parents to scoundrels. They forced poor Phil to play his violin on the streets of New York until he had earned at least two dollars. All he could keep was three cents for a bit of bread, and he was beaten if he hadn't brought back the full amount."

"Beaten?" She shook her head in disbelief. "It's just a story. Isn't it? It didn't really happen."

"It's a story about something that does happen." I opened to the first page. "Right here Horatio Alger tells show he came to know about these boys." I explained the beginning of the story as I flipped through to a part that would be simple to follow and started reading aloud.

"He beat me sometimes," he answered.
"Beats you? What for?"
"If I bring little money."
"Does he beat you hard"
"Si, signor. With a big stick."

Theresa was listening intently. I put the book in her hands and said, "Skip the words you don't know. Just remember it's only a story, but there are children like Phil. If you have any questions you can ask me."

I left her, staring at the page I had opened to. When I looked in half an hour later she was frowning, her lips moving as she read. She didn't even know I was there.

My aunt asked me that evening, "Theresa seems distracted lately. Is anything wrong between her and Tom?" As I told her why and how I was teaching Theresa to read, and the book I had chosen, Delia nodded approvingly. When I finished she said, "You would have made a good teacher, Mary."

I took her words as a compliment at first, but they lingered in my mind. Why had she said, *"would have made?"* I could be a teacher in Ireland. I didn't need Girls' Latin or Boston University. I could go to Queen's College in Galway.

∞

I pictured myself taking Mrs. Dinsmore's place someday, a very pleasant picture until I remembered a recent article in *The Boston Pilot*. Crops were failing in Ireland. Many Irish were still leaving for America. If the times were so hard, would a lot of families be paying Reardon's store in eggs, chickens or vegetables?

Uncle Pat and Aunt Aggie would find it hard to save for Jamesy, Maggie, Lizzie, and now the twins. I couldn't expect them to save for me.

CHAPTER 37

From that night on, Delia and I never referred to the bitterness that existed between herself and her mother. Instead, staying on safer grounds, we talked about her early years in Boston. I learned that she'd barely made a living, working first for a dressmaker, then for a milliner. Not until she came to the Wooleys as parlor maid had she felt secure.

Although I could almost see and feel the past she described so vividly, I had no idea how she felt about the present, and we never talked about my leaving..

As Mrs. Wooley's weekends in Chestnut Hill stretched to three and four days at a time, we had hardly enough to keep us busy. Delia went out many afternoons but didn't suggest that I go with her. I took long walks, and watched the flowers open on the forsythia and breathed in the fragrance of purple and white lilacs. When the tulips in the Public Garden lost their petals, I told myself that I'd be in Ballydare by the time the fuchsia and rhododendrons were in bloom.

I was always back before Delia returned, usually carrying a hatbox. I'd often hear her rummaging in the attic and wondered if she was looking forward to using my room again for her hat-making. I didn't ask, because I didn't want to hear her say yes.

Some nights I dreamed about ships and tossing waves. Once I woke and couldn't fall back to sleep. The dream felt so real. As Aggie separated brown eggs from white, Uncle Pat waited on a customer, and Jamesy swept the floor. Then Maggie came in carrying one of the twins. Gran followed with the other, Lizzie hanging onto her apron strings. I went to each one, offering to help, but they all smiled and shook their heads.

I woke with a start. Gran was happy with her other grandchildren. She didn't need me. And when I returned, I'd be a niece in a house already over-flowing, where nobody really needed me.

I lay awake until pigeons cooed in the eaves, and early light outlined the edges of the window shade, then got out of bed. As I washed my face in the basin on my dresser, I was surprised by my reflection in. the mirror. I hadn't even known I'd been crying.

CHAPTER 38

That evening, as my aunt hemmed a dress she was making for my trip, she said, "When I heard the direction the horse trolleys would be extended, I took all my savings and bought a building lot in Brookline. After I'd sold it for three times what I'd paid, I asked Mr. Wooley's advice on what to do with my profits."

"Mr. Wooley must have been impressed," I said. I knew I was.

"Impressed enough to offer to hold a mortgage on any property I considered a good investment." She looked at me over the top of her glasses.. "No bank would have backed a woman, let alone an Irish Catholic woman. The week before he died, I promised to stay on as long as Mrs. Wooley needed me." She sighed. "That may not be too much longer. She seems to be happier every time she spends a few days in Chestnut Hill. I expect that, with her son's coaxing, by next winter Sabine Street could be closed. Cissy will be happy to go there and be with Andrew. Marie will certainly have a better kitchen. It will all be for the best."

I had a sinking feeling. Everything in Boston would be moving on without me. It would change and go on as if I'd never been there. "Won't you miss living in the city?" I asked. I couldn't imagine Delia away from the shops and libraries.

"I won't be going with them," she answered firmly. "I've kept my promise." She hesitated a moment, then handed me the dress. "Have Mrs. Rafferty run over this with an iron in the morning.

You'll be coming with me tomorrow"

I draped the un-ironed dress over the back of a chair in my room, hoping that she was finally taking me to a store to see one of her hats for sale.

∞

It was almost noon when my aunt and I stepped into heat as uncomfortable as the afternoon I arrived. But instead of heading toward the shops, we crossed through the Public Garden in a direction I wasn't expecting. We must have walked away from the downtown area at least twenty minutes before turning down a side street. Delia had lapsed into the silence of a few weeks back. At a stretch of narrow brownstone buildings, she stopped in front of a house with a gleaming black door and a gleaming brass knocker. Bowed windows extended to the top floor.

Delia pointed up t he stone steps. "I bought this house over a year ago, in the event that-" She didn't finish the sentence, and I followed her through the newly painted front door with no idea what event she meant.

The hallway was dark, but sunlight flooded through the window of a front room. "I should have drawn the blinds," Delia said opening one window, then another.

As my aunt fussed with her hair nervously, I said, "It's a nice house."

"I could sell it today for more than I paid for it."

"Is that what you're planning to do?"

"No." She opened a door, and we passed through a smaller room into a back room. Two long tables held the feathers and braid and ribbons from the attic.

"You're going to live here when Mrs. Wooley moves to Chestnut Hill. You're going to open a hat shop!" I exclaimed. "That's wonderful."

She shook her head. "For awhile I'll continue selling to the stores. Maybe I'll open a hat shop." She ran her hands over the sides of her hair although there wasn't a strand out of place. With a final pat she said, "Come see the rest of the house."

We climbed the narrow staircase to the second floor, where she flung open a door to a sun filled bedroom with flowered paper almost identical to Ellen's room. The dresser, bureau, and bed were garlanded with painted roses, less intricate than Ellen's, but with as nice an effect.

Before I could catch my breath, Delia said, "If you decide to come back sometime for a visit, Mary-" Her voice broke, then she continued in a matter of fact tone. "Or if you decide to return with me at the end of the summer, this is your room. It was to be a surprise, but-"

It was hard to take it all in. The room. Return with her?

"I've booked passage on the *Halcyon*. I'll be going back with you. For a visit."

I caught my breath. "Going back! Together!"

My aunt smiled. "Yes, together."

For a moment we were both speechless. Then she walked to the window and stared down at the street. Still speechless, I joined her and watched the people below, walking purposefully, yet pausing to greet each other. A girl my own age entered a house across the street. It was a neighborhood of families, as Sabine Street must have been before the younger people moved away to places like Chestnut Hill.

"I tried to write my mother a letter," Delia said without turning. "I'd start, but I couldn't put it in words. Going back is the only way. We leave the twentieth, and you'll have the whole summer to decide what you want to do. I'll understand either way. There'll be no hurt feelings."

She left the room quickly. I heard her moving about downstairs, and knew she wanted to be alone. I pulled a small chair into the bow of the window and leaned against the sill looking absently now at the passersby. And thinking. Delia had bought the house long before she'd written to Father Sheehy. From the day I arrived, she'd been furnishing my room, saving for the day when we could leave the Wooleys and live in this house. She hadn't told me any of this, until she was sure I *wanted* to stay with her.

I left the window and walked around touching each piece of furniture, a lump rising in my throat, her phrase, *I couldn't put it in words*, echoing insistently. Just as she couldn't find the words to write to Gran, my aunt couldn't ask me to stay, because she couldn't put it in words.

With words, she could make the past come alive. She could

tell me exactly what a new word meant. Explain a difficult passage in a book. But she couldn't say what she felt.

It was not because she had a heart of stone. She had proven that by deeds. The hours she'd spent with me. The books she'd bought.

This house. *This room.*

I slumped onto the edge of the bed, recognizing how much we were alike, Gran and Delia and I. I'd moped in silence for weeks, hoping she would ask me to stay. Gran could tell wonderful tales about the Wee Feeneys and the Tiny Tunneys. But although she'd written regularly about my "Grand opportunity"' she'd let Delia know only indirectly how she felt.

I took one last look around the room.

It didn't have to be that way.

I ran down the stairs. My aunt was gazing out the front window. From the living room doorway, I said, "Aunt Delia."

She turned, her face a mask that showed nothing.

Standing straight, my hands clasped tightly behind my back, I said, "I love my room, Aunt Delia." And then I asked, though I guessed what the answer would be, "Is it far from here to Girls' Latin?"

"An easy walk," she answered with a smile. "And all flat, no hill."

CHAPTER 39

The next few weeks flew by. Ellen's father gave us two new leather suitcases and a steamer trunk from his attic, which we promptly filled with gifts to take back to Ireland.

A few days before we were to leave, my aunt and I stood in the front door to say goodbye to Mrs. Trottier and Cissy. As they waved happily from the carriage that was taking them to Chestnut Hill, I doubted they would ever return to Sabine Street.

Theresa had chosen to stay in the city to be near Tom. Dandy O'Connell recommended her to be a companion to an elderly Irish woman whose son had done well after opening two funeral homes. As I watched her leave with Tom the next day, in a fashionable and very likely expensive new outfit, I could hardly picture the timid girl who'd walked into Aunt Aggie's with downcast eyes, barely speaking. Since reading Phil the Fiddler, followed by two books in The *Ragged Dick* series, she had told both Tom and Dandy O'Connell that they should pass some laws to protect children. It was easy to imagine her as Theresa Kerrigan, in years to come, advising Tom what he should do as the mayor of Boston.

On the day my aunt and I were to sail, Ellen and her father came to Sabine Street. . Ellen handed me a nicely wrapped box. "It's writing paper. I want to hear all about your visit to Ireland." She hesitated. "Maybe you'll find time to write to my grandmother. I know she would like that."

"Of course," I agreed. "But not before I write to you."

Mr. Wooley handed Delia a single card. She read it aloud and laughed.

Miss Delia Reardon. Hats made to enhance the individual face.

"My wife will send cards like these to everyone she knows, when you are ready," he said. "We owe you so much for all you have done."

"It's no more than I've owed you," Delia replied.

When our belongings were inside the carriage that would take us to the dock, I looked back at the gleaming windows and the glistening brass knockers on the front door of the brick house that had impressed me so much, less than a year ago. Now I saw it as the home of old Mrs. Wooley who had spent so many years there. Marie Trottier had found it a safe place for herself and the little girl she'd promised a dying woman she would raise as her own. Theresa, in spite of the "haunts," had been happy there, learning how to run "the grand house" she and Tom were sure to own someday.

And yet, every one of us, including Mrs. Wooley, had been glad to move on. Aunt Delia and I would return to our own new home.

I took a deep breath, turned, and climbed into the carriage. Because we were heading back to my other home .

As we rode toward the dock, I ticked off on my fingers the places I recognized. The Public Garden. Boston Common. The State Capitol. The Stores on Tremont street. Belchers, where we'd had our photographs taken. Long before the carriage moved through the congested market, I ran out of fingers.

We arrived as a tender left for the waiting ship. Relatives waved from the dock. Around us, hawkers offered small American flags and candies shaped like maple leaves. An old man held out a fistful of golden pebbles with a toothless grin, saying, "Buy a bag of gold picked off the streets Boston. Give the folks back home a good laugh." Another called out, "Limes, pickled limes, for the crossing."

I smiled at my aunt. "Pickled limes. Those are what Amy ate in *Little Women*. I wonder what they taste like."'

"We'll soon see," Delia said, taking out a few coins.

As she bought a half dozen limes, I looked around the dock

noticing how much better dressed the passengers were as they returned for a visit to Ireland. No bundles tied with rope. Even their faces looked less strained.

Suddenly a stocky red-faced man jostled me, apologizing quickly, "Excuse me Miss.

I turned to say, "That's alright," but he was already racing toward a wagon marked P.J.Moriarty & Sons Fresh milk. Fine dairy products. Deliveries throughout the Boston Area."

I caught my breath. P.J.Moriarty! It had to be Petey!

I shaded my eyes with my hand from the late morning sun. Even from a distance I recognized Mrs. Moriarty in the center of the tender chugging toward the *Halcyon*.

When the tender returned, my aunt and I climbed in. As we bounced across the choppy water toward the waiting ship, Delia called against the breeze, "That's a better looking vessel than the one I came over on."

An hour later, we stood at the *Halcyon's* rail and watched the city slip away. Neither of us needed to say what we felt. We'd be happy to return at summer's end. After we passed Boston Light, Delia said, "Let's walk a bit."

I took my aunt's free hand. "There's someone I want you to meet. She's crossed the ocean eight times so she can see her children on both sides of the Atlantic."

"She must be a remarkable woman," my aunt replied, holding her feathered hat against the wind, as we walked hand in hand to the spot Mrs. Moriarty would surely be claiming as her own.

The End.

Thea Gammans grew up in the neighborhood of Boston and has lived in New York and Nashville.

She attended Radcliffe College and has been a songwriter in both New York and Nashville.

She enjoys travel and has made several trips to Ireland where she did some of her research for this book.

.

9486429R00109

Made in the USA
San Bernardino, CA
19 March 2014